I, JOHN CULPEPPER

Lori Crane

LORI CRANE

I, JOHN CULPEPPER

Published by Lori Crane Entertainment
Cover design: Robert Hess
Editor: Elyse Dinh-McCrillis at The Edit Ninja

www.LoriCrane.com

This book is a work of historical fiction.
Some names, characters, places, and incidents are from historical accounts.
Some names, characters, places, and incidents are products of the author's imagination.

ISBN: 978-0-9903120-5-5
eBook ISBN: 978-0-9903120-6-2

Praise for Lori Crane

"Lori Crane's writing is magnetic...she pulls you in with her unabashed honesty, eloquent simplicity, historical genealogical knowledge and pastoral care of each and every character."
~Amazon customer for *Okatibbee Creek*

"Lori Crane is a Southern storyteller of the first order."
~*Writer's Digest* for *The Legend of Stuckey's Bridge*

"This is a five-star book written by a five-star author."
~ Readers' Favorite for *An Orphan's Heart*

"Crane writes with great attention to detail and an authentic historical feel." ~Christoph Fischer, award-winning author of *The Luck of the Weissensteiners* and *Sebastian*

"As always, Ms. Crane delivers a great story.

Descriptions are precise, the dialogue flows easily, and the characters are well rounded."
~ Anna Belfrage, award-winning author of *The Graham Saga*

"This is a five-star winner and Lori Crane is a must-read author."
~ Readers' Favorite for *The Legend of Stuckey's Bridge*

Table of Contents

Family Lineage/Cast of Characters

Family Patriarch: John Culpepper of Wigsell Manor 1530-1612

John's son:
Sir Thomas "Tom" Culpepper of Wigsell 1561-1613
Tom's sons: Slaney Culpepper 1598-1618
               John "JC" Culpepper 1599-

John's son:
John "Johannes" Culpepper of Astwood 1565-
Johannes's wives: Ursula Woodcock 1566-1612
               Eleanor Norwood 1570-1624
               Ann Goddard 1590-
Children: Thomas Culpepper 1602-
          Cicely Culpepper 1604-
          John Culpepper 1606-
          Frances Culpepper 1608-

John's son:
Sir Alexander Culpepper of Leeds Castle 1570-
Alexander's wife: Mary St. Leger 1550-
Mary St. Leger's son: Warham St. Leger 1579-
Warham's daughter: Katherine St. Leger 1602-

I, JOHN CULPEPPER

CHAPTER 1
Fall 1626

"No! For the hundredth time, no!"

John looked down at the intricate grain of the walnut desk beneath his fingertips and shifted his weight to his other foot. He sighed, feeling his dreams disintegrate before his very eyes. The snap of the white sails, the taste of the salty spray on his lips, the smell of the tar that sealed the decks—the visions were quickly vanishing behind the thick fog of his father's adamant disapproval. He pictured his mighty ship sinking into the black waters of condemnation, bubbling like a cauldron as it disappeared from sight. There was nothing he could do to change his father's mind, and he wondered whatever possessed him to come to this man for assistance. He should have known better.

His father glared at John from behind the desk. He propped his elbow on the scrolled arm of the chair as his large hand methodically stroked his pointed beard. "Is there anything else?" he snapped.

John didn't look up. He shook his head and mumbled, "No." He turned and padded across the thick rug toward the door, listening to the man's heavy breathing behind him. He reached for the brass doorknob, paused, and turned back. "You know I've always done everything you've asked of me. I went to school. I studied to be a lawyer. I did it all for you. I never wanted to practice law. I'd never be happy on the bench."

"Happy? What makes you think life has anything to do with being happy? You are a Culpepper, and as such, you have an obligation to serve your family and your king in a manner befitting your station. This childish notion of owning a ship is nothing but rubbish."

John released the doorknob and walked back toward his father's desk. The intimidating man dwarfed the desk, his size exaggerated by the broad shoulders of his leather jerkin, yet he sat up taller in his chair in preparation for the quarrel to continue. It was a wasted gesture, as his opponent already knew the battle was lost.

John made sure he didn't raise his voice. "Father, you have financed merchant ships for as long as I can remember. What difference does it make if I'm the one who owns the ship?"

"Culpeppers don't own ships. I funded those expeditions as an investment—a losing investment, I might add." He rose from his chair and his voice grew louder, echoing off the oak panels that lined the walls. "There has never been a Culpepper placed in a position of experiencing hunger and savages and shipwrecks, and there won't be one now, not with my blood written on the purchase. I will not fund a ship for you, John, not now, not ever." He pointed his finger in John's face. "And if you somehow find a way to procure a ship, mark my words—I will disinherit and disown you. No son of mine will become a common sailor. I am finished with this conversation once and for all. Have I made myself clear?"

John exhaled, beaten. His shoulders slumped as he broke his father's glare and dropped his eyes to the floor.

"John? Have I made myself clear?"

"Completely."

CHAPTER 2
Twenty Years Earlier, 1606, Blackwall, London

"Master Culpepper! Master Culpepper!" the servant boy shouted over the bells clanging from the church steeple. He pulled the scratchy scarf tightly around his neck to ward off the chill as he pushed his way through the masses gathered on the foggy banks of the Thames.

The crowd had been gathering on the wharf for nearly two days to witness the departure of the ships, and they were prepared for a spectacle unlike any they had seen before. When the tide came in, the three ships carrying one hundred forty passengers and sailors would depart England on an exciting adventure. The air smelled of salt and tar and sweat. This was a remarkable place, a magical place, where the preparations were as exciting at the coming voyage. The anticipation in the air was nearly as thick as the fog.

The boy stopped for a moment as a wooden cask was rolled across the cobblestone in front of him. He watched as workers carefully rolled the barrel up the tilted gangplank. He remained frozen in the middle of the bustling crowd, staring at the ship. He had never seen anything so majestic in all his twelve years, and his jaw dropped at her sheer size. She was an enormous castle-like structure, at least eighty feet in length, her belly bulging at the side where the last of the cargo was being loaded in. Crates and boxes were continually being carried up the gangplank, where they disappeared into the ship's dark interior. The deck above the cargo area was much narrower and the boy imagined that's where the sailors would remain during the voyage, climbing masts and hoisting sails. Circling the spiderweb of hemp ropes and yardarms, seagulls cawed as if singing along with the rhythmical clanging of a nearby metal object. The boy scanned the scene for the source of the sound and noticed a blind beggar sitting on the cobblestone near the bow of the ship, tapping a stick on a metal bowl.

Behind the ship floated a second ship, nearly as large as the first, and behind that loomed a third. Each hosted its own cast of sailors, supplies, vagrants, and gangplanks. As wavelets gently raised and lowered the vessels, moans of protest arose from the taut ropes, and the weathered wood creaked with each stomp of a sailor's boot. Nearby, two mangy hounds barked and growled over some fish scraps, bringing the boy's attention back to his task at hand. Remembering why he had come, he yelled, "Master Culpepper!" He spun around and around looking for the man, weaving between horses, carts, trunks, and sailors shouting commands. He darted in and out of the crowd, making sure he didn't bump into any wealthy gentlemen, recognizable by their long cloaks adorned with colorful silk threads.

In April, King James had created the Virginia Company, which would finance sailings to Virginia and Plymouth with the aim of settling colonies and profiting from the land's abundant natural resources. The aristocracy funded the expeditions with the expectation of making an exorbitant profit. The three ships embarking from Blackwall on this day would sail to Virginia and bring back riches. There were rumors of gold, silver, and gems merely washing up on the shore for the taking. If nothing else, there was surely timber to be harvested. The trees in England had long been felled and the rising price of timber would certainly bring the investors a hefty return.

After they finished loading supplies and the morning fog had dissipated, the ships would raise their sails and ride the tide down the Thames. They would enter the English Channel and cross the great ocean and return by summertime.

The boy bobbed in and out of the crowd, searching for his master.

"Who are you searching for, lad?" a man in a ruffled collar asked.

"Master Culpepper," the boy replied, removing his hat and revealing his dirty blond hair, which was sticking this way and that like a wheat field in a mighty windstorm. He twisted the wool hat in his hands.

"Johannes or Tom?"

"Johannes Culpepper, sir."

"I saw him down by the front ship—the *Discovery*—only moments ago. He was standing right on the dock."

"Thank you." The boy nodded, replaced his

cap, and shoved through the workers and onlookers toward the front ship. As he passed the first ship, he looked at the name written on her side and sounded out the letters. He couldn't make any sense of the words *Susan Constant*, but when he reached the second ship, he could read *God...speed*. He wondered if the *Godspeed* was true to her name. If he were to sail, he would rather sail on the *Godspeed* and get there faster. From what he understood, it was a two-month voyage if the weather was bonny, maybe four months if the ship ran into rough seas.

He had once spent a morning in a small fishing boat and instantly became green with sickness that lingered for several days. He didn't think he would be able to survive the time it would take to sail to Virginia. He gawked at the bow of the *Godspeed* as he ran past, witnessing a young lad about his age. The sailor dripped with sweat, even in the chill of the damp morning air, as he coiled ropes and folded sails. What a great adventure it would be to sail to Virginia, but alas, the boy would never get to do such amazing things. He was a servant, a gift from His Majesty King James I to Johannes Culpepper. He would always be a servant, but perhaps someday he would be fortunate enough to serve the king. Even though Master Culpepper was good to him, he wished to someday live at court and be somebody. At least he had the slimmest of chances. His sister had been placed in the kitchen of some castle in Wales. She would never be anything more than a scullery maid. Women would never hold a place in society. They were not welcomed on this voyage, either.

He hopped up and down, unsuccessfully

trying to look over the crowd. "Master Culpepper!" he called.

A man turned and pointed. "Culpepper is right over there, son."

"Thank you, sir."

The boy sprinted in the general direction, and when he pushed through a couple workers conversing on the dock, he saw him.

"Master Culpepper!"

The boy ran up behind Johannes Culpepper and patted the back of his master's arm, hopping up and down. "Master Culpepper!"

Johannes turned and looked down at the boy, his square jaw set and his blue-gray eyes burrowing into the lad. "What is it, boy? Why are you making such a commotion?"

The boy panted, out of breath from running. "Master Culpepper, m'lady is havin' the baby, sir!"

Johannes's face turned red as he glanced around the crowd to see if anyone was eavesdropping. When he saw no one was, he folded his arms across his chest and stroked his beard. "You came all this way to tell me that?"

"Yes, sir."

"Very good, boy. You run along home now."

The boy didn't move. How could his master not be excited about this news? Did he not want to return home and see his wife and child? Was there anything the boy could say to convince the man to accompany him back to the house?

"Go on. Run along." Johannes waved the boy off with a flip of his ringed fingers and abruptly turned his back.

"Yes, sir." The lad backed up, keeping his

eyes on his master, wondering what he would tell the governess when he returned home without his master in tow. He had ridden nearly four hours to get to Blackwall this morning, most of it in the dark as the sun had not even risen when he left. He would have a four-hour return trip to think of something. He turned and walked back in the direction from which he had come.

Tom gave Johannes a hardy pat on the back. "Congratulations, brother! Hopefully another fine son."

Johannes grunted, narrowing his eyes at the ship before him. "I wouldn't count on it."

Tom laughed his usual robust laugh, attempting to lighten the mood. "Oh, what's bothering you? You should be happy."

Johannes didn't respond.

Realizing his joviality wasn't working on his grumbling little brother's mood, Tom wiped the smile from his face. "Do you want to head home to see how Ursula is doing?"

"No," Johannes barked and shook his head, his dark curls swaying as he did so. "I want to stay here and guard my investment. These ships need to set sail and bring back the treasures of the colony. It doesn't matter if I have a son if I don't have anything to leave to him when I die."

"But you already have young Thomas. He will inherit your lands and manors."

"Yes, but I need a spare in case anything happens. Thomas has been weak and sickly his whole infancy, and after Ursula gave me a daughter the last time, I'm not getting my hopes up. I want to stay right here until these ships have sailed."

Tom nodded. "Very well, brother. We shall stay."

Not another word was said about the coming child as the Culpepper brothers watched the great ships cast off their lines, raise their sails, and float down the Thames. The crowd cheered and waved at the departing ships until the vessels had sailed around the bend and disappeared from sight.

CHAPTER 3
Later That Day

Tom gently placed his mug of ale down on the scarred wooden table and wiped the corner of his mouth with his knuckle. "So, are you going to head home in the morning?"

Johannes curled his lip and shook his head. His eyes scanned the crowded Blackwall Inn. The horde had been celebrating and drinking since the ships set sail earlier that morning, and they had gotten increasingly louder with each passing hour and pint of ale. He leaned across the table toward his brother and raised his voice over the noise. "No, I have to oversee the reading of a will in the morning, and in a few days, I'll need to witness the signing of the new deed for the heirs."

"Your work never ceases, brother. What about Ursula?"

"What about her? The governess is with her. I'm sure she's fine."

"And what about the babe?"

"What about it?" Johannes groused. His eyes kept scanning the room as if he was looking for someone.

"Aren't you anxious to see if it's a boy or a girl?"

Johannes rolled his eyes. "What difference does it make? Do you expect me to abandon my business dealings here in London and run home just because my wife has a child? What if it *is* a girl? I can't shirk my commitments to my clients, especially for a girl." He took another swig of warm ale from his mug and winked at someone across the room. The slightest grin crossed his lips and a dimple creased his cheek. His eyes twinkled with mischief.

Tom knew that look. He followed Johannes's gaze and saw his brother was unashamedly flirting with the redheaded wench who waited tables at the pub.

Johannes took another drink, gazing over the rim of his mug at the redhead. "Besides, I have better things to occupy my time for the next few days."

Tom shook his head. "You should be a little more discreet, brother."

"Why? Everyone knows my wife has been with child, and everyone knows I have desires that need to be met. It's certainly no secret."

Tom raised his hand to the barkeep, indicating he'd like two more pints. "Well, I'll have one more drink, and then I need to take my leave and get some sleep. Unlike you, I am going home to my wife and children in the morning, and Father needs me at home. Since Uncle Martin's death, he hasn't been doing so well."

Johannes looked back at Tom. His eyes narrowed and the first signs of his thirty-one years showed in faint wrinkles around his eyes. "I heard

Father was ill. Any idea what's wrong with him?"

Tom waited to answer until after the burly barkeep had plopped two full mugs on the table, oblivious to the amber ale sloshing over the rims and onto the wood. As he lumbered away, Tom replied, "I don't know what's wrong with him. It could be a real illness or maybe just melancholy over losing his brother, but he's an old man, so anything could be life threatening at his age."

"Oh, he'll be fine. He's always been resilient. I'm sure he'll be back to his robust self soon enough." Johannes took a drink and cocked his head. "I know what you're up to. You just want to stay close to him to make sure you're in his will."

"That's not true," Tom playfully snapped.

"Oh, yes, it is. You did the same thing last year when Uncle Martin fell ill, and so did our little brother, but Uncle Martin didn't leave either of you the estate you wanted, did he? Unbeknownst to you both, he had already promised Astwood Court to me."

Tom sat up straight and wagged his finger toward his brother's face. "Contrary to your beliefs, little brother, neither Alexander nor I were ever interested in owning Astwood Court. Why would I want that house when Father is going to leave me Wigsell? And why would Alexander want it when he has a place as amazing as Leeds Castle?"

Johannes threw his head back and laughed. "Yes, Alexander's house is something, eh? Marrying St. Leger's widow was the best thing our little brother's ever done."

"Yes, but she's a beautiful woman as well, so he is certainly lucky all the way around."

"Beautiful woman? She's twenty years his senior. The old hag has a son the same age as Alex." Johannes gulped his ale.

"Alexander married her for love."

"Love of her money," Johannes said. He took another drink and leaned back in his chair.

Tom sighed, knowing full well Johannes's wife also came from a very wealthy family. "We all have our immoralities, Johannes. Anyway, my point is, neither of us wanted Astwood Court so your presumptions are incorrect. I don't understand why you want that house out in the country anyway. It's more than a week's journey from London. Isn't Greenway Court a lot more convenient for your business? That house is so close, even your young servant boy made the trip alone this morning, and he's probably already back home by now."

"Of course Greenway Court is convenient, but when I receive my fortune from this Virginia expedition, I think I should like to retire to Astwood and become a true country gentleman."

Tom leaned back in his chair, laced his fingers across his chest, and chuckled. "I certainly can't see you retired, brother. What would you do with yourself all day, sitting around idle in the countryside? Watch the trees grow?"

Johannes stared across the room at the redhead and grinned. "I think I could find something to occupy my time."

Tom sat up straight and placed his elbows on the table. His face became more serious. "Do you really think we'll make a profit on this investment?"

"I'm certain we'll make a sizeable return. At the very least, we should expect large shipments of timber. That will bring us a healthy yield."

The redheaded lass walked around their table and playfully rubbed her bottom against Johannes's back as she squeezed between his chair and the patrons standing at the bar. He looked over his shoulder and stretched his arm to grab her but she was already out of reach. She glanced back and smiled seductively.

Tom swallowed the last of his ale and placed his mug on the table. "Well, there are no barmaids in the country, brother."

Johannes followed the girl's movements with his eyes. "Maybe I'll take that one with me."

"I'm sure Ursula would have an opinion about that." Tom walked around the table and hugged his brother good-bye. "Congratulations again on the new child, and when you find your way home, send word on how Ursula and the babe are doing. I'll see you soon."

Johannes patted Tom on the back. "Safe travels, brother, and give Father my regards. Tell him I'll come out to Wigsell and see him soon."

Tom nodded and then weaved his way through the drunken patrons as he exited the noisy inn, leaving Johannes alone to find a way to occupy the rest of his evening.

CHAPTER 4
John Culpepper

"Good afternoon, Master Culpepper," Mrs. Woodbury greeted Johannes as he stomped in the front door of his estate. Greenway Court, comprising only nineteen rooms, was the most modest of the family's many manors, yet still a magnificent three-story mansion, complete with formal gardens, acres of plough and pasture, wood and heath, and more than a few dozen head of sheep and cattle.

The productive and profitable estate required a staff of over two dozen to keep things running smoothly, and none of the servants was more loved and respected than the governess, Mrs. Woodbury. She had moved in with the family when Johannes and Ursula's first child, Thomas, was born four years earlier. She was a plump, middle-aged widow, with gently graying hair and warm chocolate eyes, who held no greater love in her heart than to oversee a family. Her husband had died nearly a decade earlier and the last of her own children had grown, married, and moved away, so she found herself alone and in need of income. At the recommendation of his father, Johannes hired Mrs. Woodbury as the governess and she was very, very good at her job. Johannes and Ursula loved her and treated her as one of their own.

"Good afternoon, Mrs. Woodbury." Johannes distractedly removed his hat and held it toward her as he looked down at the correspondence piled high on the foyer table.

"Welcome home, m'lord. How was your trip?" She reached for his hat and held her arm out for his cloak.

"Productive." He handed her his cloak, picked up the stack of letters, and began sorting through them.

"Your wife has delivered you a fine son, m'lord." She shook the dust off his cloak. When he didn't respond, she said, "A healthy and bright-eyed boy."

He turned and looked at her with no expression.

She rested his hat on top of his cloak and dusted it off while she waited for him to say something.

Finally, he placed the letters back down on the table and rubbed his thumb and forefinger on his beard. "A son, eh?"

"Yes, m'lord. He's quite a strong lad. Takes after his father, I suppose," she chirped as she turned and shuffled from the room, clicking her heels across the tile floor.

He watched her robust frame waddle through the doorway. Her news had considerably brightened his day. *A son. Let's hope he's stronger and more virile than Thomas.* Johannes sighed. *I guess the only way to find out is to go upstairs and see for myself.* He climbed the massive staircase and tapped lightly on his wife's bedroom door.

"Come in," she called.

He pushed open the heavy door a few inches and peeked through the crack. The room was dim with all the heavy curtains drawn. It was quite different up here than the sunshine-filled bustle of the rest of the house. The room was quiet and warm, with the soft flickering light of candles dancing on the tapestries that covered the walls. He called out, "Ursula?"

"Johannes? Is that you? Please, please, come in."

Her golden voice was as sweet as an angel's, and that made him smile. He'd married her because of her cheerful voice—well, that and her family's money. The Woodcock family had more manors and land than the Culpeppers, and the time-honored tradition of marrying heiresses and widows was generally the way the Culpepper men gained their fortunes. But Ursula had something else about her that Johannes loved. She was warm-hearted, with a gentle smile and soft manner. He had initially been attracted to her by the way she said, "Good morning," and "Good evening," and particularly the way she said, "Johannes." Words floated from her lips as if they were lyrics she was singing just for him. Her voice had a happy lilt that filled his heart the way nothing else did. Today, it made him happy to be home.

He swung the door wide, entered the lavishly appointed room, and found Ursula sitting up in the four-poster bed, wearing a soft white gown that floated over her petite frame. A stack of pillows rested behind her back and her legs were covered with a brightly colored velvet quilt. Her hair was plaited on either side of her face, and Johannes was momentarily awed by how peaceful she looked. Childbirth agreed with her.

Her expression was one of excitement and anticipation as she held their newborn in her arms, and her smile grew more radiant as he approached the bed. "It's a son," she said.

"I heard. Very good work, my dear." He walked around to the far side of the bed and looked at the bundle in her arms.

She gently placed the infant on the quilt and removed his swaddling so Johannes could get a better look at him. Not the slightest whimper or cry escaped the infant's lips as Ursula removed his wraps.

Johannes studied the babe, leaning over to gaze at him in the dim candlelight. The curly-headed boy was robust, not broad shouldered but still well proportioned. His arms and legs moved with determination, as if he had somewhere important to go. Johannes touched the babe's tiny clenched fist. The child grabbed his finger and wouldn't let go. Johannes laughed in surprise.

"He's got a nice strong grasp," he said.

At the sound of Johannes's voice, the babe opened his eyes and looked at Johannes. Time stood still as the two gazed at each other for what seemed like an eternity. Johannes admired the clear, attentive eyes that stared back at him. Blue eyes, like his own.

"He has the Culpepper blue eyes and curly hair. We should name him after his grandfather. His name shall be John, and he will be the third generation of lawyers in the family. John Culpepper, Esquire."

A tear of happiness ran down Ursula's cheek at her husband's pleasure with this new son. Ursula looked down at the babe and whispered, "John Culpepper." She looked back at her husband. "It's perfect."

Johannes brushed back a strand of Ursula's dark hair from her ivory temple. He leaned down and kissed her on the forehead. "You have given me a very respectable son, wife."

Mrs. Woodbury rapped on the open door and entered the room, carrying clean bedding and gushing over how beautiful the baby was.

Ursula said, "Mrs. Woodbury, my husband has named the child John Culpepper."

"Oh, that's a strong name for a strong boy. He shall be a great brother to Thomas and Cicely, and I suspect he shall grow to be a great man, just like his father."

CHAPTER 5
July 1611, Wigsell Manor

"Let's run!" five-year-old John yelled to his older brother Thomas.

"No!" shouted Ursula, but it was too late. The boys had already jumped from the moving carriage and were running across the lawn of the massive estate, heading toward their grandfather who waited at the top of the stairs in the arched doorway of Wigsell Manor. Ursula chastised them and asked Mrs. Woodbury to make them behave respectfully, but there was not much the women could do. The boy's excitement could not be bridled. They galloped through the formal garden gracing the twelve-hundred-acre estate, hopping over flowers and darting around hedges.

Above their grandfather loomed the three-story manor, its roof shielded in tile that covered three finial-topped gables housing attic windows in their centers. Stone chimneys graced either side of the enormous house, as well as a row of chimneys rising from the back of the roofline.

"There are my boys," exclaimed their

grandfather, opening his arms wide to greet them.

"Grandfather!" John yelled as he ran.

When they reached the elderly man, he wrapped them in a long hug, exclaiming how much they had grown and how much he missed them. Their young cousin, Katherine, hid in the doorway, shyly peeking around the corner.

Katherine hardly knew her cousins, as she lived at Leeds Castle with Alexander Culpepper. When the youngest Culpepper son, Alexander, married Anthony St. Leger's widow eight years earlier, he was also blessed with her grown son, Warham, who was nearly Alexander's age. Warham was a ship commander who led expeditions for months and sometimes years at a time, and while he sailed, his young daughter, Katherine, lived at Leeds Castle with her grandmother and stepgrandfather, Alexander. Since Alexander had no children of his own, the girl quickly became the great joy of his life. As she grew, he adored her even more. She was a beautiful child with a complexion of ivory surrounded by silky auburn curls and green eyes the color of emeralds. On this afternoon, those green eyes watched from the safety of the doorway as John and Thomas greeted their grandfather.

"Did your father come with you this visit?" the old man asked the boys.

"No," they answered.

"He had to work in London," explained Thomas.

"Of course he did. He always has to work in London. Well, you tell him he should come visit his old father."

"We will, Grandfather," Thomas said.

The old man ruffled Thomas's hair. "Well, we'll have a good time regardless. Why don't you run along to the back terrace and greet your uncles."

He turned to the small girl. "Katherine, why don't you take the boys back to the terrace?"

He watched the children race through the house until they were out of sight. He smiled at their energy and excitement.

The carriage rounded the circular drive and slowed. When the old man's redheaded servant appeared behind him, he instructed the servant to assist the ladies from the carriage and help the footman unload the family's trunks and place their belongings in their usual rooms. The young servant nodded and descended the stairs.

When the carriage came to a stop, the footman jumped down from the back and placed a step on the ground in front of the door. The servant opened the door and offered his hand. Ursula took it and emerged from the carriage into the sunlight that shimmered on her green satin gown. Her dark brown curls peeked out from under her matching bonnet. She smoothed down her dress with her gloved hand and looked up at the house, grinning at the old man waiting at the top of the steps.

Seven-year-old Cicely followed behind her, ignoring the servant and jumping over the step. Her curls bounced on her shoulders when she landed on the ground. She ran past her mother and jumped up the steps to greet her grandfather. She hugged him quickly and ran into the house to chase after her brothers.

Mrs. Woodbury emerged from the carriage next in her black dress, grunting as she stepped down. In her arms, she held the youngest member of the family, three-year-old Frances. The child was sleeping soundly against her governess's ample bosom.

The elderly man slowly descended the steps and greeted the ladies, warmly hugging Ursula, kissing Frances on the forehead, and nodding hello to Mrs. Woodbury. He instructed his servant to escort Mrs. Woodbury inside, where she could lay down the sleeping child.

Mrs. Woodbury, a bead of sweat on her forehead, waddled up the steps as she followed the servant into the house. The driver and footman disappeared behind the carriage to unload the family's belongings. Ursula and the old man found themselves alone in the driveway. They hugged again.

"I'm so glad you're here, Ursula. How was your journey?"

"It was uneventful, but I'm glad to have a few moments of silence here with you. Those children love to talk and John loves to tease his sisters. I must have scolded him twenty times."

"He's quite precocious, eh?" The white-haired man laughed.

"You could say that."

"How long can you stay?" he asked as he offered his arm to escort her.

"We'll stay the entire month." Ursula entwined her arms around his elbow and they strolled together across the stone drive toward the house. The redheaded servant jogged past them back toward the carriage. "The children are so excited to play on the grounds and spend time with their cousins. Was that Katherine I saw on the porch with you?"

"Yes, Alexander is on the back terrace enjoying a pint of ale with Tom."

"Oh, I didn't know Alexander would be here. That's so nice."

"They arrived yesterday. Wait until you speak with Katherine. She's the brightest little thing and such a joy."

"How old is she now?"

"She's about the same age as your Thomas…nine, I suppose."

"Well, I'm glad they're here. It'll be nice to visit with them." She stopped walking and scanned the shrubs and flowers that lined the front of the house. "Everything looks good."

"I have Tom's boys tending the garden. Gives them something to do over the summer."

"Yes, I guess they're old enough to learn the responsibilities of the estate."

The old man thought for a minute. "Yes, JC is twelve now. That would make Slaney thirteen. I say, Tom has his hands full with those two. Rebellious Culpeppers through and through."

"They can't be much worse than my boys, especially John." Ursula giggled. "For all the trouble your sons caused you while growing up, you must find some solace knowing they're getting it all back raising their own boys."

He chuckled. "Yes, it makes me laugh when I see them frustrated with their sons. Serves them right for being so rebellious in their youth and turning my hair gray." He walked toward the house and looked up at the clear late afternoon sky. "What a beautiful evening. I'm glad you arrived before dark."

"I'm glad, too. Hopefully the weather will remain pleasant. All the boys talked about all the way here was going fishing."

"I'm sure they'll get some fishing in during their visit."

When they reached the house, Ursula released his arm, lifted her skirt a few inches, and climbed the stairs. He hobbled up the steps behind her. He paused for a moment in the doorway to catch his breath, and Ursula turned back to see why he was delayed. He looked pale.

"Father, are you ill?" she asked.

"No, no, my dear. I'm just old. Plain and simple."

She smiled. "Oh, nonsense."

"I'm eighty, my dear. A considerable age, don't you think?"

"Eighty? My word, that certainly is considerable." She offered her arm to escort him inside.

"Well, don't you worry about me. I'll live as long as Methuselah. What about you? How are you doing? I hope that son of mine is treating you well."

"Of course he is, and he is so pleased with his sons. Their tutor says they're both incredibly smart." They walked arm in arm through the lavishly appointed hall, passing paintings and marble statues, her skirt making a soft swishing sound with each step.

"Of course they're smart. They're

Culpeppers." He chuckled, then became melancholy. "I wish Johannes had come with you. I haven't seen him for such a long time."

She patted his arm as they passed through the library, heading toward the back terrace. "I know, but you know Johannes. He always has work in London. He said he'll be able to join us in a few weeks after he finishes some important business."

"He's a good lawyer."

"Yes, he is, Father. Yes, he is."

* * *

"We never catch any fish in this pond," complained John as he sat with his slack line bobbing in the water. His dark curls rested on his forehead, shining like silk ribbons in the high noon sun.

The four boys fished at the pond in the middle of their grandfather's property every summer. They had ventured down to the pond every day for the last two weeks, but they hadn't caught any fish as of yet. Thomas and Slaney sat on one side of the pond and John and JC sat on the other.

"I don't think there's any fish in this pond," John said.

"I don't think so, either," JC said. He then yelled toward the other side of the water at Slaney and Thomas, "Have you caught anything?"

"Only grass from the bottom," replied Slaney.

Even with no fresh fish in their bucket, the boys enjoyed the warm days of summer. They sat on the banks with their breeches rolled up and their bare feet dangling into the cool water. All four lines lay motionless across the top of the pond as they tried unsuccessfully to entice the fish.

John stared at the water, watching the reflection of the clouds drift by in the summer breeze. "Why do they call you JC?" he asked. He had been learning letters from his tutor and was just beginning to spell words. "I just realized the letters J and C don't spell anything."

"Those are my initials."

"Why do you use initials? Why don't you use your real name?"

"Because my real name is John Culpepper and that's our grandfather's name."

"Your name can't be John Culpepper. That's *my* name."

"Exactly. It's also your father's name, but they call him Johannes."

John counted on his stubby fingers, frowned, and shook his head. "There are four John Culpeppers?"

JC laughed. "Yes, Grandpa, your father, me, and you."

"Oh." John gazed across the pond for a moment, his forehead wrinkled as he tried to figure out how someone else could have his name. "I guess JC is a good name for you, then," he concluded.

JC stood up and skipped a flat stone across the surface. "I won't be called JC forever, though. In a few years, I shall go to Oxford, and then study law at Middle Temple just like our fathers did. I plan to serve His Majesty in Parliament, and Father says someday I'll inherit his shares in the Virginia Company and then I can retire as a country gentleman. But what I'd really like to do is work for the king as a knight." He waved an imaginary sword through the air. "Then I will be called *Sir* Culpepper."

"You sure do have a lot of plans." John reeled in his fishing line and noticed there was no bait on the hook. "A fish must have nibbled off my bait." He handed the fishing pole to the servant standing nearby. The servant placed a wiggling worm on the hook and handed the rod back to John. John plopped it back into the water. "Will I have to call you Sir Culpepper after all that happens?"

JC laughed. "No, you can still call me cousin."

"Good." John grinned, showing his missing front tooth.

"Boys! Boys!" Mrs. Woodbury bounced down the hill, flushed and out of breath.

"What is it, Mrs. Woodbury?" Thomas responded from across the pond.

"Thomas, John, your father has arrived. Clean yourselves up and come greet him."

The boys rushed to dry their feet and put their stockings and shoes back on. They left their fishing poles in the care of the servant as they ran up the hill.

* * *

That evening, the children dined with Mrs. Woodbury while the adults sat down to supper in the elegant dining room of the manor. The cook served a spectacular meal of pheasant and spiced bread, and the group shared more than a few bottles of French wine. The table was full of lively conversation and merriment, with the elder John Culpepper enjoying the company of his three grown sons and their wives. It was rare for the family to gather in one place, and they were all happy to see each other.

After they finished the main course, Johannes tapped his knife on his crystal glass to get everyone's attention. The clinking of the glasses and plates died down as everyone looked at Johannes, who announced, "I'm glad everyone is together tonight, for I have some exciting news for you all." He paused and took a drink.

The family remained silent while the servants brought in the desserts and placed a dish in front of each person.

When the servants finished, Tom asked, "So, what is your news, brother?"

Johannes smiled. "I'd like to announce that I am taking my family and moving to Astwood Court." Johannes drank alone as the rest of the family stared at him.

Ursula's jaw dropped. She didn't take her eyes off her husband, but she could feel the rest of the family looking from his face to her face, wondering who would speak first. She finally broke the silence. "But that's so far away, dear."

"Yes, it is, wife, but I have decided to give up my law practice and become a true country gentleman."

Alexander now reached for his wineglass. "Give up your law practice?" He gulped his wine and held the empty glass in the air for the servant to refill.

Johannes nodded and looked at Tom. "I

would like you to take on all my clients."

"Well, um," Tom stuttered. "I guess I would be happy to do that, brother."

"Good. It's settled, then. We shall leave tomorrow and travel straight to Astwood."

"What about our belongings? Greenway Court has been our home for ten years. We have so much to pack," Ursula said.

"We don't need to pack. We'll send for our things." Johannes dug his spoon into his pudding. "From now on, I shall be a gentleman of the country, and I look forward to spending more time with my family." He looked around the table awaiting everyone's approval, but none came. The whole family was accustomed to him working long hours and being away from home for weeks at a time. Ursula looked down at her plate. Tom eyed Johannes warily. Every member of the family was skeptical about how long this retirement would last.

* * *

As the morning sun warmed the countryside and glistened on the grass's dewdrops, John and Thomas were hugged extra hard and long by their grandfather. "It will probably be a long time before I see you boys again," the man said sadly.

"Why, Grandfather? We come here every summer and every Yuletide," Thomas countered.

"Yes, but you're moving far away now. I'm not sure you'll ever come back here."

John's face darkened. "Moving far away? To where?"

"Your father is moving your family up to

Uncle Martin's estate, a place called Astwood Court. You'll like it there. It has a pond just like the one here."

"I don't want to move," said Thomas. "What about our house?"

"I don't know what your father will do with Greenway Court. All I know is you boys are headed to Astwood, where you will live in great splendor." The white-haired man smiled, his wrinkles deepening around his blue eyes as he did so.

He knelt down on one knee and pulled John close to him. "Young man, I know you're too young to understand this, but I may not see you again. Astwood is very far away."

"How far?"

"At least a couple weeks by carriage. But I want you to promise me you will be good."

John nodded.

"You will study hard with your tutor."

He nodded again.

"And you will always follow your heart no matter where it takes you. Be brave and fearless, and I promise you, the future has great things in store for you. Know that I love you and will always watch over you, even when I'm gone."

"Where are you going, Grandfather? Are you moving, too?"

"No, lad, I'll be right here." The old man chuckled. He struggled to rise back to his feet, and when he did so, he patted John's head.

The boys ran toward the waiting carriage, smiling and waving good-bye.

The old man stepped down the front steps, following the carriage as it rolled around the drive.

He crossed the stone drive and stepped onto the wet grass, the last of the morning dew soaking through his slippers. When the carriage rounded the end of the drive and he couldn't see it any longer, he turned and slowly walked back to the steps. When he reached the top step, he stopped and turned around, hoping to see the carriage returning but knowing that would not be the case. He sighed and looked down at his damp slippers. With great sadness, he entered the house and closed the door.

CHAPTER 6
1612

The arrival at Astwood Court was not without its spectacle. The carriage entered the grounds through two ancient oaks and crossed an enchanting bridge spanning a moat. Birds sang from high in the treetops and squirrels darted in front of the carriage. The gravel drive followed a gentle curve around the property. Landscaped lawns spread on either side of the drive, interspersed with formal gardens and mature trees of ash, cherry, and chestnut.

From the carriage window, Ursula saw an apple orchard and behind that, the stables. Though she had not been happy about the move, when she saw the house for the first time, with its shaped soffits and gable ends, she softened considerably. It was lovely. The entry was shielded by a covered porch, and the massive front door led directly into three handsome reception halls. Flagstone floors, beamed ceilings, and quaint inglenooks with enormous fireplaces welcomed the family to their new home. The boys ran around and around the reception rooms, while Ursula took Cicely by the hand and walked past them into the large kitchen. Double doors led to the breakfast terrace, and Ursula smiled as she and Cicely looked out the door's windows to the gardens outside. Ursula opened the doors and the cascading sunlight warmed the large kitchen. This was her favorite place in the house thus far. On the far wall stood a single wooden door with no window. She watched Johannes open it and look out into the side yard.

"The stable is out this way," he reported and disappeared outside.

Mrs. Woodbury, carrying Frances, peeked around the door and viewed the large barn and the small chicken coop.

Two small servant's staircases stood at either end of the house, leading up to the first and second floors and down into the cellar, whilst a third staircase in the center of the home, which was to be used by the house's residents, led up to the family's quarters. The manor was indeed grander than Ursula had imagined.

In time, the family's possessions were delivered to their new home, and the Culpepper family settled in nicely.

The following year at Astwood Court passed without incident, but when summer warmed the countryside with its lazy days of sunshine, Ursula took ill. Her slender frame was racked with fever and pain, and she didn't emerge from her room for more than two weeks. The entire family, as well as the staff, was greatly concerned.

"Mrs. Woodbury, did the doctor come this morning?" Johannes asked one day as he entered the kitchen, stomping his boots on the rug.

"Yes, m'lord. He was here while you were out at the stables," she replied as she pounded some dough on the wooden table. A white cloud of flour shrouded her head.

"What did he say about my wife?" Johannes walked toward the table.

She wiped her hands on her linen apron and shook her head. "He said there's nothing he can do for her. Her skin is hot as burning coal and she has developed a cough of blood. He said she is suffering from consumption and that she has probably suffered from it for some time." She looked at him as she tried to summon the courage to continue. "I knew she had been fatigued the last few months, and I asked her about her cough a few times, but she insisted she was fine. The doctor said..." Her voice cracked and she stopped. She took a deep breath. "The doctor said she will likely expire very soon, m'lord." She looked down at the mound of dough as a tear fell from her eye.

Johannes didn't move from the edge of the wooden table for a long time, staring beyond it into the fire that roared in the stone fireplace. His thoughts spun. Perhaps the doctor was mistaken. He wondered if he should call in another doctor. Ursula couldn't possibly be sick enough to leave him a widower with four small children to tend. His wife, his darling Ursula—she had never done anything to anyone. She was the kindest woman anyone would have the pleasure to know. She didn't deserve this illness, and he certainly didn't deserve to bury his wife. *No, this has to be a mistake.* He clomped out of the kitchen and hurried upstairs.

He pushed open the heavy door that moaned

in protest on its rusty hinges. "Ursula?" he whispered.

A maid who was sitting by Ursula's bedside answered. "She's sleeping, m'lord."

The room was dark with all the curtains drawn. Moments ago in the stable, with the sun filtering brightly through the barn doors, he had just delivered a healthy calf. The animal had immediately risen from the hay-covered floor and tried to walk, taking unsteady steps toward its mother. Here, inside the bleakness of a dark room, his wife was dying. This was not the way life was supposed to be.

He took a few steps toward the bed and the sight of her pale face nearly stopped him. She looked as white as the sheet she was lying on. He walked around the bed and sat in the chair next to her, taking her hand in his. She was burning with fever. She looked so frail, he was afraid he would hurt her if he squeezed her hand, so he simply allowed it to lie limp in his own. The maid sat on the opposite side of the bed, sponging cool water on Ursula's forehead and down her wilting arms.

"Would you like me to leave, m'lord?" the maid asked.

"No, that's all right."

Ursula's eyes fluttered at the sound of his voice.

"Ursula?" he said softly.

She looked at him, trying to bring his face into focus, and coughed faintly. A trickle of blood seeped from the corner of her mouth and the maid quickly wiped it away with the damp cloth. Dark circles surrounded her eyes that seemed more black than brown, and she was emaciated. It broke his heart to see her like this.

"Johannes." She moved her lips in a barely audible whisper.

He longed for her familiar lilt, but knew he would never again hear her beautiful voice. He would never again hear her singing to the children or calling his name. She closed her eyes as her forehead wrinkled in pain. He watched her, not knowing what to do. "Ursula, you mean so much to me. You've given me four beautiful children and filled my life with twelve years of happiness."

She whispered, "Watch…over…the children."

He nodded and gently wiped her damp forehead, pushing a stray lock of her curls back from her temple. "Of course I will."

Another weak cough escaped her lips and the maid again wiped the blood from her mouth. Johannes rose and bent over to kiss Ursula on her forehead. The grimace on her face vanished as she exhaled. Johannes sat back down in the chair and watched her for a long time, waiting for her next breath, but it never came. The maid quietly rose and left the room, sobbing as she closed the door behind her. A few minutes later, Mrs. Woodbury entered the room to confirm that her mistress was dead. She stood across the bed from Johannes, shedding silent tears.

"M'lord, I'm very sorry. She will be greatly missed by all of us."

Johannes didn't respond. After a few minutes, he rose and sighed heavily as he wiped his hands across his face. "I'm going into town to take care of some business. Will you tell the children?"

"Sir, I'm sure they'd rather hear something like this from their father."

"No, I can't." His voice sounded almost panicked. "Please tell them, and I'll be back later tonight."

He left the room.

After a few moments of sitting alone with her mistress, Mrs. Woodbury rose from her chair and gently kissed Ursula's hand. "Goodbye, m'lady."

She wiped her face with her palm and left the room to see to the tasks that needed to be done. She called on the servants to begin cleaning the room and preparing the body, and she went to find the children.

Once she had them all seated in Johannes's oak-paneled office, she gazed sadly at them, not knowing how to begin. Thomas, now ten years old, sat on a cane chair with four-year-old Frances on his lap. Cicely, with pink satin bows holding her brown locks, knelt on the floor in front of them. Six-year-old John sat on the far side of the room in his father's big chair behind the desk. Mrs. Woodbury had always admired how John was different from the other children, but at this moment, she wished he would sit closer to the group so she wouldn't need to speak any louder than necessary.

Quietly, she said, "Children, I have some very sad news to tell you." Their frightened faces almost broke her heart, but she continued. "I'm afraid your mother has died." She didn't know what else to say, so she remained silent and waited for the words to sink in.

It didn't take very long. Cicely's eyes filled with tears and a sob escaped her throat. She jumped up and ran to Mrs. Woodbury, wrapping her arms around the governess's waist and burying her face in her hip. Frances was too young to understand the gravity of the situation, but the sight of Cicely crying frightened her and she began to cry also. Thomas wrapped his arm around her as tears rolled down his own cheeks.

"Died?" little Frances asked, as softly as a squeak from a mouse.

"Yes, child. I'm afraid she was very, very sick."

Mrs. Woodbury remained still and allowed the children to grieve. As she stroked Cicely's hair, she watched John stare out the window across the room. The boy didn't say a word. He didn't shed a tear.

After a while, Thomas asked, "May we see her?"

Mrs. Woodbury nodded. "Of course you may." She held out her palm toward Thomas, motioning for him to come with her, and she took Cicely's small hand in her own. Thomas stood and put Frances on the floor. She reached up for his hand and together they walked toward Mrs. Woodbury. John didn't move.

"John? Don't you want to come with us?" Mrs. Woodbury asked softly.

John turned toward Mrs. Woodbury, his face red and his eyes narrowed, filled with tears. Not of sadness, but of anger. "Why would she die and leave us all alone?" he snapped.

Mrs. Woodbury released Cicely's hand and walked over to John. She fell to her knees in front of his chair and took his ice-cold hands in her own.

"She didn't leave you because she wanted to, dear boy. She loved you with all her heart, but she was very sick. And you're not all alone, John. You have your father to look after you. And you have me. I'll never leave you."

John pursed his lips. "My father doesn't look after me. He's never even here."

She patted his knee. "He does the best he can, child."

"Well, where is he now? Why are you telling us that our mother is dead? Why isn't he here telling us? If this is the best he can do, it's not good enough."

Mrs. Woodbury's shoulders drooped. She knew John was right. Everyone knew that. But there was nothing she could do. John snatched his hands away from her. He jumped up from the chair and ran past her, out of the room. A moment later, footsteps pounded down the staircase, followed by the slam of the front door. Mrs. Woodbury shook her head and sighed. Using the corner of the desk for leverage, she rose to her feet and turned to the waiting children. "Come, children. I'll take you to see your mother now."

* * *

A few weeks later, a horse galloped onto the property. Its rider was the redheaded servant from Wigsell Manor. The stable boy met him outside the barn and took the reins of his horse.

"Where can I find Johannes Culpepper?" the servant asked as he dismounted.

"This time of day, he'd be in his office, I

suppose. Knock on the back door and Mrs. Woodbury will instruct you," answered the stable boy.

The man hurried across the lawn toward the back of the house and was greeted at the kitchen door by the round woman he had seen at Wigsell on many occasions.

"Hello, Mrs. Woodbury. I have an urgent message for Master Culpepper from his brother at Wigsell Manor."

"Oh, I hope everything is all right." She waddled across the kitchen floor and called over her shoulder. "Wait here, lad, and I'll see if m'lord can greet you."

When she returned, she was wringing her hands. "Young man, please follow me. M'lord asked that you come upstairs to his office."

She led the servant up the main staircase and knocked lightly on Johannes's office door before opening it. "M'lord, your visitor," she said as she gestured for the servant to enter. She then closed the heavy door behind him.

The young man nodded to Johannes and handed him a folded piece of paper. The front read *Johannes Culpepper*. The back was sealed with a red wax stamp from Wigsell. Johannes broke the symbol, unfolded the stiff paper, and read.

My dearest brother,
It is urgent that you come to Wigsell at your earliest convenience. Our father is not well and may not wait long for your arrival. Please make haste.

With deepest love,
Your brother,
Tom Culpepper

Johannes pushed his way past the servant as he ran out of the office and galloped down the stairs, all the time yelling for Mrs. Woodbury, who had gone back down to the kitchen. By the time he reached her, his face was flushed and he was out of breath. "Mrs. Woodbury, pack the children at once. We're going to Wigsell immediately." He stomped across the kitchen floor and out the back door, leaving it open as he hurried across the yard toward the stables.

She followed him into the yard and yelled after him, "Is everything all right, m'lord?"

"My father is dying!"

* * *

The children were excited to visit Wigsell, but the two-week journey was quite an ordeal for them. The family's ornate carriage was followed by two coaches filled with servants and supplies, and the caravan's occupants spent uncomfortable nights sleeping in the carriages and on the ground, as Johannes was in a great hurry and would not veer from the road to find an inn. Neither he nor Mrs. Woodbury told the children why they were unexpectedly traveling to Wigsell, but the children recognized the adults were very tense. They had never visited their grandfather's house in the fall, and John knew deep in his heart something was amiss.

When they arrived at the great manor, the carriage wheels crunched across the newly fallen leaves. Uncle Tom emerged from the stone archway that graced the front of the house. He looked ashen and distraught, with deep lines of concern on his face and dark circles surrounding his bloodshot eyes. John jumped down from the coach before it came to a stop, and bolted across the browning lawn. He ran past his uncle and jumped up the steps into the house, yelling for his grandfather.

He stopped abruptly inside the doorway. All the heavy curtains were drawn. The entry hall was dark and gloomy.

"Grandfather!" John called as he ran into the parlor. A single lamp glowed on the table in the corner, casting dim shadows on the ornate walls and carved ceiling. The fireplace was dark. No one was there. John turned and ran across the hall into the library. "Grandfather!" That room was also dark.

"John," his uncle Tom called.

John exited the library and walked back toward the front door.

His uncle approached with hands palm up, pleading for John to come to him. "I'm afraid your grandfather's been very ill. Please don't yell for him."

"Ill?"

"Yes, he's…" Uncle Tom dropped his hands and looked at the floor.

"I want to see him," John demanded.

"That's probably not a good idea," his uncle said softly as Johannes marched through the front door, passed them both, and took the dark walnut staircase two steps at a time.

"I want to see my grandfather!" John yelled

and ran after his father.

"John!" his uncle called after him.

John didn't stop moving, but when he reached the landing halfway up the staircase, he looked back toward his uncle. From his perch on the staircase, he saw his siblings enter the front door, holding hands with a pale Mrs. Woodbury. He would not stay here with them. He would see his grandfather, and he would do so at this very moment.

When his father opened the door to Grandfather's room, the stench almost brought John to his knees. *What is that smell?* He quietly entered the room, staying in his father's shadow as they neared the bed. The room was dim and the curtains were tied back to the posts of the elegant four-poster bed, which was surrounded by people. John scanned the faces and recognized his uncle Alexander, some servants, and one man in a black robe whom John knew was a bishop. The bishop was waving a round metal object over the bed and delicate puffs of smoke were rising from it. That's what that smell was—some sort of incense. The servants parted as Johannes neared the bed. John peered around his father's waist and witnessed a frail, old man lying on the bed, propped up by pillows and covered by a brown blanket. He stared at the pale, skeletal figure, barely recognizing his own grandfather.

The bishop mumbled something in Latin that John didn't understand.

A man spoke to Johannes. "You must be his son. I'm Dr. Newson. I'm sorry, he just died a few minutes ago. You're too late."

No one else said a word or moved. They all

stared down at the man on the bed. John replayed the doctor's words in his head. Died? Too late? It was as if all the air had been sucked out of the room. John looked from face to face, waiting for someone to say something, anything to help him understand what the doctor had said.

"I'm sorry, brother," whispered Tom, who had entered the room behind them and taken his place at the foot of the bed. Tom then looked down at John and said, "He died while he was sleeping, boy. There was no pain. He just stopped breathing."

Except for a young maid weeping in the corner, silence again filled the room, and tears began to fill John's eyes.

"No!" John screamed at the top of his lungs, startling everyone in the room. "He can't die!"

John pushed his way around his father and crawled on top of the bed, straddling his grandfather's stomach. He grabbed two fistfuls of the old man's nightshirt and started shaking him. "Grandfather! Grandfather! Wake up!"

Johannes grabbed him around the waist and pulled him from the bed. "John, stop!" he said firmly.

The old man's nightshirt ripped from John's grasp as he kicked and struggled against his father. Tears streamed down his cheeks as he kept screaming for his grandfather and Johannes carried him from the room.

CHAPTER 7
Yuletide 1617,
Astwood Court

As the cold winter evening continued to drop a soft blanket of snow onto the lawns and gardens of Astwood Court, Slaney and JC arrived from Oxford University for the Yuletide festivities.

Following their grandfather's death in 1612, Wigsell Manor had been left to their father, but one year later, Tom died suddenly in a hunting accident when he was thrown from his horse. Upon his death, the manor was left in the keeping of his brothers until Tom's eldest son, Slaney, attained the age of twenty-one, an event still two years away. Johannes and Alexander had decided it would be best for the boys to move to Oxford University after their father's death and begin their studies, just as Tom had wished. Over the next four years, the boys had never once returned to their childhood home. The grand estate sat cold and empty this season, just as it had for the last four winters. Slaney and JC spent every Yuletide at Astwood Court with Johannes's family.

The boys entered the house, the front door flying open wide as the wind caught hold of it. John ran to the entry hall to greet his older cousins. "It's about time you arrived. I was afraid the weather would delay you another day." He hugged JC and then Slaney.

"Sorry we're so late," JC said as he stomped his snowy boots on the rug.

"The roads are slippery so we had to keep the horses at a deliberate pace," Slaney added.

"How are you, young John?" JC asked, brushing snow from the shoulders of his cloak.

"Very well, cousin. How are you? How is Oxford?"

"School is fine, or I should say *was* fine. We've both finished our studies, and we are now alumni of Oxford University," JC answered as he removed his cloak and hat.

Mrs. Woodbury approached the boys with a smile and her chubby, calloused hands extended. "Good evening, boys. Let me take your cloaks."

The boys greeted her warmly.

Johannes appeared around the corner. "Ah, you're here! Happy Yuletide to you, nephews."

"Happy Yuletide, Uncle," they said in unison.

Johannes gestured toward the parlor. "Come. Sit by the fire and warm yourselves. How was your journey?"

"Uneventful, Uncle," said JC.

"Looks like you made it just in time. The snow seems to be piling up out there."

Johannes's wife, Eleanor, and the rest of the children appeared in the parlor within minutes. They hugged the boys and welcomed them. Three years after Ursula's death, Johannes had found love again at the age of fifty and married forty-five-year-old Eleanor Norwood, the widow of Sir George Blount of Sodington. Her seven children had grown and married, and with her history and experience as the lady of the Blount estate, she was more than capable of running Astwood Court. She had easily stepped into the role of mistress of the Culpepper household, commanding servants and doting on the Culpepper children as if they were her own. She had effectively turned Astwood Court into the warm home it had not been since Ursula's death.

The family sat in front of the roaring fire, catching up on the latest news from London. Within a few hours, the conversation moved to the table in the dining room, where the kitchen staff had prepared a magnificent feast. Platters overflowed with plum pudding, cakes, breads, cheeses and apples, and the table's centerpiece, peacock. Goblets were filled to the rim with wine. The conversation was lively and animated as Johannes listened to all the details of the boys' schooling.

"So, JC, do you still plan to go to Middle Temple?" asked Johannes.

"Yes, Uncle, I am to start in February."

Johannes took a bite of cheese and washed it down with wassail. "And what about you, Slaney? Are you going to attend Middle Temple also?"

"I would like to, if that would be all right with you, Uncle. I don't see any need to return to Wigsell right now. I would really like to graduate as a lawyer."

"I think that's a wise thing to do, Slaney," Johannes agreed. "The estate will still be there when you finish school, and you'll be in a much better position to manage it once you get some law experience. Law practice is something this family is very good at, and I know your father would be immensely pleased if you would follow in his footsteps."

"Well, you've watched over Wigsell for a long time, but if you wouldn't mind, would you please continue for another few years until I've finished school?" Slaney asked.

"I'd be happy to do so. That's what the family elder is for," Johannes assured him.

Thomas and John had been admiring their older cousins, who seemed so mature and worldly, unlike themselves. They had seldom been beyond the property lines of Astwood Court and had not experienced the amazing things in London that JC and Slaney had.

Thomas piped up. "What about me, Father? Am I to attend Oxford and Middle Temple someday?"

"You're not old enough to attend either," his father replied.

"Not yet, but I will be soon."

"We'll discuss it then, son."

Thomas pouted and dug his fork into the bird on his plate.

Slaney looked across the table at John, who was sucking on a plum he had pulled out of the pudding. "What about you, John? Do you want to go away to school?"

"No. I want to own a big ship and become a merchant."

"A merchant?" JC laughed. "Why would you

want to do a thing like that?"

John sat up straight and looked JC squarely in the face. "I think ships are beautiful, and I want to do something no one in the family has ever done before. I want to sail across the ocean and be an adventurer."

Everyone at the table chuckled. John looked at each family member, wondering what was so funny.

JC spoke up. "Young cousin, Culpeppers don't do that sort of thing, although Uncle Alexander's stepson, Warham, is currently heading an expedition for Sir Walter Raleigh. They sailed to Guiana to search for gold, but I heard they ran into some problems with the Spanish."

"Raleigh should still be imprisoned in the Tower where he belongs. I don't know why the king let him out after he was found guilty of treason." Johannes shook his head.

"The king let him out so he could go find El Dorado's gold," Slaney said.

"Well, getting Warham involved in that futile quest is unsettling," Johannes continued.

"Warham has always been an adventurer. I'm sure Raleigh didn't have to beg too hard to convince him to go," JC said.

"It's a good thing Warham's using St. Leger money instead of Culpepper money to fund Raleigh's expedition. I know from years of experience that sailing is nothing but a losing venture. Your father and I lost more money than I can count financing the Virginia Company. We sent dozens of ships to Virginia and they never returned with enough goods to even pay back our initial investment," Johannes added.

"I shall like to be like Warham St. Leger and sail a ship," John said.

"Don't you want to study law like the rest of us?" JC asked.

John shook his head, his dark curls bobbing on his shoulders. "I don't need to know the law to command a ship."

Johannes folded his napkin and dropped it on the table. "Well, there you have it—my son, the rebel." He pushed his chair away from the table and laughed, but his laugh held more frustration than humor. He beckoned Mrs. Woodbury to come and take the children to bed. While the cousins bid each other a good night, Johannes dismissed himself from the room and poured himself a large glass of wine in the parlor.

Mrs. Woodbury escorted the children up the stairs, and when John reached the landing, he turned back to witness his father offering JC and Slaney a glass of wine. The fireplace glowed warm in the front room and John wondered if he would ever be old enough or important enough to be offered a glass of wine and share conversation by the firelight. He wondered if he would ever enjoy the camaraderie his cousins shared with his father. Considering the man didn't even say good night to him, he figured that day would never come.

CHAPTER 8
September 6, 1620,
London

Fourteen-year-old John stood on the banks of the Thames and stared at her. She was the most majestic creature he had ever seen. He admired her pear shape, her curved lines. From the beak of her prow to the tip of her stern, she must have been nearly one hundred feet in length. Three masts towered above her decks and her white sails billowed, straining against their ropes. Fluttering atop her mainmast, the red-and-white English flag proudly announced her pedigree. She rode the gentle waves toward the English Channel, sailing into the rising sun. Her sharp silhouette stood in contrast to the backdrop of a clouded pink-and-purple sky.

"What are you looking at, boy?" his father bellowed from the carriage.

He pointed at the river as he turned. "Look at the ship, Father!"

"Stop gawking and get over here and unhitch these horses."

"Yes, sir," John mumbled. He trudged back toward the carriage, wondering why there wasn't a footman or stable boy to take care of the animals. He walked around to the other side of the horses and wrapped his fingers around one of the halters.

He peeked around the horse's nose, watching his father march through the puddles as he crossed the road toward the inn. His father's long black cloak billowed behind him, caught by an unexpected breeze. John looked up at the sky. Last night's storm clouds were dissolving and large pockets of blue sky were beginning to show through. When he looked back at his father, the man's shadow was walking beside him, just as formidable as the real man.

Thomas appeared by John's side and plopped their father's large trunk on the ground at John's feet. The horse jumped and John quickly released the halter.

Thomas complained under his breath, "You'll never learn, will you? That's not one of our ships sailing for the Virginia Company. That's a competitor's ship. Father isn't interested in that ship. As a matter of fact, Father has lost so much money investing in these expeditions, he's not interested in any ships or your fascination with them."

"How much money?"

"What?" Thomas asked from the back of the carriage, where he was now retrieving another trunk.

"How much money has he lost?"

"I don't know exactly, but he's been waiting for shipments of timber from Virginia that never arrived. He said the men who sailed there were too busy trying to survive to cut any trees. So, each time a ship returns empty, Father loses money."

"But money aside, how can he not love them? All of them. They're beautiful. Imagine where that ship is heading, sailing off to some enchanted seaport. Silk from the Orient, cotton and tobacco from the colonies. I can picture it coming ashore in Virginia, where one can view rolling land as far as the eye can see, so much land and it's nearly free for the taking." John turned to gaze again at the ship as it rounded the bend of the river. He took a step away from the horses so he could see her better, if only for the next few moments until she disappeared.

"Don't admire that ship too fondly. She's not going to the Orient. She's called the *Mayflower* and she's going to Plymouth." Thomas looked at the ship. "And she's not so grand. As a matter of fact, she's rather old. She's already crossed the ocean quite a few times." He looked back at John. "And why are you talking about rolling land? You'll never own land." He laughed as John struggled with the horse's buckles. "Father will leave everything to me. You will be sent to Middle Temple to be trained as a lawyer, and someday you will oversee my estates."

John gave up on the buckles and marched toward his brother. "I don't want to oversee your estates. Oversee them yourself. You're the one who wants to go to school, not me."

"I don't think Father is planning to send me to school." Thomas pouted as he untied the last of the trunks from the back of the carriage. "He wants me to become a country gentleman, the next in line to manage the Culpepper fortune. I shall remain at Astwood Court and you shall go to London and attend Middle Temple."

"Well, I don't want to do either. I don't want to live in the country, and I certainly don't want to go to some stupid law school. I want to sail, on a beautiful ship like that one." He looked again as the *Mayflower* was completing its turn around the bend. He could only see her stern.

"John Culpepper!" his father bellowed from the front door of the inn. "Stop daydreaming and get to work!"

John turned, took a step toward the horse, and focused on the buckles. "Yes, sir."

Later that evening, John brought up the subject of ships with his father. His father was stern in his reply.

"John, I don't ever want to hear you bring up this subject again. Being on a ship is no place for a Culpepper and it would be a disgrace to our family. No son of mine will sail across the ocean for nothing but a fool's dream. Stop speaking as if you were a commoner. You will never own a ship, you will never sail on a ship, and you will stop gawking at every ship you see. Do you understand me? You will become a lawyer and serve our family and the king, just as our men have always done."

"But, Father, what about Warham St. Leger?"

"Well, his name says all there is to say. He is not a Culpepper."

CHAPTER 9
January 14, 1621,
Theobalds Palace

John walked behind his father and his brother as they passed through an ornate room containing a colossal fountain crafted of black and white marble. Water trickled down the sides of the fountain and splashed into the basin. John looked down at the splatters on the marble floor and carefully stepped around them. His father called to him to keep up and he hurried forward. While standing in line to enter the Queen's Chapel, he looked up at the arched ceiling and noticed the beautifully carved timber. The windows of the gallery faced south and the afternoon sun blazed into the room, causing all the adornments to glimmer as if gilded with gold.

The trio entered Queen's Chapel and John sat on a bench between his father and Thomas. He looked around at the lavish decor and windows of stained glass. Colorful tapestries of hunts and battles decorated every wall, and magnificent chandeliers floated from the twenty-foot ceiling. All the seats were soon taken and the growing crowd, bejeweled and wearing their finest garments, lined the walls. There were many knights and barons in the Culpepper family, and as John looked from face to face, he counted over a dozen of his kin in attendance. His excitement increased as JC entered the chapel through the arched doorway and walked to the front of the room. A hush fell over the crowd.

JC had graduated from Middle Temple and would now be knighted by His Majesty King James I. John had never witnessed anyone receiving a knighthood, certainly not a member of his own family. It was all happening exactly as JC had predicted ten years ago at their grandfather's pond. From now on, JC would be known as Sir Culpepper. John couldn't be prouder.

It may not have happened if Slaney hadn't died in December of 1617. The year the boys entered Middle Temple, Slaney took ill, and no matter what the physicians did, his condition kept deteriorating. Slaney never attended a single class. He lay in bed, withering away for eleven months, and then expired, leaving JC as the sole heir to the Wigsell fortune. King James, wishing to repay the Culpeppers for their loyalty and service, wanted to grant knighthood to the brightest and best of the Wigsell line of the Culpepper family, and that distinction fell upon JC.

The trumpets sounded and everyone rose for the king's entrance. He marched through the arched doorway. He wasn't wearing his crown, as it wasn't a royal event, but he donned a red velvet hat and looked just as stately as if he were wearing the crown. As JC had done only moments before, the king passed through the standing-room-only crowd, but this time everyone bowed and curtsied. As they bowed, their expensive fabrics made a swooshing sound with each step the king took, and John wondered if he ever grew tired of that noise. It sounded like a wave washing through the room. When the king reached the altar, the archbishop told everyone to be seated and summoned JC forward to take his oath.

John couldn't hear all of the promises JC had to make, but he did make out the parts about being loyal to the king, devoted to the Church, charitable to the poor, and brave in the face of battle. JC then knelt before the king, who dubbed him Sir John Culpepper, Knight, with a tap of a sword on each shoulder. JC received the sword and kissed the King's ring. After a prayer by the archbishop, JC rose and turned to face the room. The crowd erupted in applause.

Following the ceremony, the crowd gathered on the sunny grounds of the palace to eat and drink and be entertained by a joust. The king had recently enlarged the park, placing a brick wall around the twenty-five-hundred-acre property. He had a tiltyard constructed in the center of the grounds, with room to accommodate at least five thousand spectators, though only a fraction of that was in attendance today.

John sat under a brightly colored canopy, his elbows resting on the table in front of him. He was flanked by his father and Thomas, and they enjoyed a feast of pastries filled with cod liver, bream, and eel. John had just finished devouring a large chunk of venison when the trumpet's blare announced the beginning of the festivities. He watched the proceedings with great enthusiasm, as he had never witnessed such a spectacle.

A knightly duel generally consisted of three jousts, the winner being the best two of the three, but none of the competitions had made it to three thus far. The goal of the joust was to break the opponent's lance and disarm or unhorse him, but the first few competitions had ended with the loser being unhorsed and assisted from the tiltyard with a squire under each arm, too battered to continue. In one case, an unconscious knight was sprawled facedown on a stretcher and carried off the field by the king's men. The crowd cheered for each victor and moaned for each loser.

Trumpets sounded again, causing the spectators' din to increase in pitch. Knights' horses were usually escorted onto the field by a groom, but a massive black horse, its face covered with metal plate, galloped onto the tiltyard. On its back sat a knight clad in iron armor, sunlight glinting on his breastplate, making it look as if it had been polished for weeks just for today's event. The crowd roared and rose to its feet as the black horse pranced back and forth, kicking up dust. The rider removed his helm and waved to the crowd. It was JC! John rose to his feet and cheered loudly for his cousin.

A second knight in full plate, riding a white horse, galloped toward the field. The crowd applauded even louder for this contestant, and John bobbed up and down on his tiptoes to see over the standing spectators. Who was this newcomer to receive more applause than his cousin? The horse was wearing plate on its face and chest, and its back was covered with a sapphire blue blanket. It was followed by a small donkey ridden by a squire carrying a standard and trying unsuccessfully to keep pace with the knight and his mighty horse. As the two approached the tiltyard, John saw the standard boasted the royal crest. It was the king!

The two opponents met each other in the middle of the tiltyard and tapped their lances together. JC nodded to the king and then pulled sharply on his horse's reins. The massive beast stepped backward and curled one of his front legs beneath him in a regal bow. The spectators gave a collective roar of approval.

The opponents took their places at either end of the field and donned their helms. The crowd's clamor dampened in nervous anticipation. Upon the herald's cry, the two contenders galloped toward each other at lightning speed, and the crowd again cheered loudly. Thunderous hooves met with hard ground, pounding like war drums of an invading army. John couldn't believe JC would attempt to unhorse the king, but the two were traveling at such an unbelievable pace, he might do so by accident. When the riders met in the middle, the crack of wood against metal made John gasp. JC splintered his lance on the king's shield, and the king was declared the winner of the first round.

The men returned to their respective starting points and JC's squire handed him a second lance. When the challengers were ready, the horses charged again. Dust rose behind each competitor as the horses thundered toward each other. This time, JC wrapped his lance around the king's and disarmed him. Half of the crowd cheered, the other half booed.

Whoever won the third battle would be

declared the winner of the match.

JC and the king returned to their places and readied themselves to ride again. John watched a young maiden throw a flower toward his brave cousin. JC nodded toward her and flashed a charming grin before lowering his face shield. At the herald's cry, the two men again charged. The closer they drew to each other, the louder the crowd cheered. The riders clashed with an explosion of wood and armor, and JC again broke his lance on the king's shield. The king was unsurprisingly declared the winner. JC dismounted, removed his helm, and bowed deeply before the king.

The nobles and gentry gathered that evening for dancing in the ornate ballroom of the palace. John watched JC standing in the corner chatting with some young maidens and was awed by his charm with the ladies. When JC noticed him, he waved John over and dismissed the ladies. They giggled and looked over their shoulders at JC as they walked away.

"So, how did you like the joust?" JC grinned.

"It was great! I bet you could have taken him."

"Shhh. Nobody declares victory over the king."

"Yes, I know, but I bet you could have."

"That will never happen." JC leaned against the wall and took a gulp of wine from his goblet. He scanned the room and raised his glass to a group of girls who were smiling at him.

"Do those lasses think you're something special now?"

"I *am* something special now, little cousin. I

am Sir Culpepper, Knight of His Majesty King James I."

John smiled. "Do you remember the summer we went fishing at grandfather's pond and you told me you would become a knight someday?"

"Of course I remember. It's the only thing I ever wanted to be."

"Well, you've done it. Congratulations."

"Thank you, John." He sipped his wine. "What is it that you plan to do with your life?"

"I told you. I want to be the captain of a merchant ship."

"Ah, yes, I remember you saying so. I thought you would have outgrown that childish notion by now."

"It's not childish, JC. It's the only thing I've ever wanted, but now since you've done so well for yourself, my father says he is going to send me and Thomas to Middle Temple."

"I spoke with your father about that today."

"You did? What did he say?"

"He just said you and Thomas would be attending very soon."

"I'm not excited about it in the least." John looked around the room. Women in elegant dresses were being spun around the dance floor by men in stylish suits. Musicians played from the corner, and servants weaved about the room filling wineglasses. "Can I ask you a question about Middle Temple?"

"Sure," JC said.

"Did you like it there?"

JC shrugged. "It was all right. I admit the study of law is a rather tedious endeavor, but it's not all studies, if that's what you're worried about. Many students are more inclined to bestow themselves on gambling and harlots, and some students are rakes with hot tempers. They absorb themselves in all sorts of fooleries, but some students are very witty. You'll figure out which ones are which soon enough. One thing is for certain, they only admit the brightest and most ambitious students, so you'll be in the company of high-minded individuals who enjoy verbal sparring more than anything else."

"I think Thomas is one of the brightest you speak of, but I think they only allowed me admittance because of my father's money."

"That's nonsense, cousin. You have always been a bright boy. In some ways, you are much smarter than Thomas. You'll do well there. You will also make good social connections. There are many members of Parliament who socialize there and lawyers who live and work at the Inn. You'll know them by their bawdy flowing ringlets and the latest ruffs and cuffs. One word of advice, little cousin…"

"What's that?"

"Stay away from the headmaster. His name is Barnaby and he is intolerably wicked."

"How wicked?"

"If you're tardy for your lesson, he will threaten to expel you, but he can't actually do that because the school would lose too much money from men like your father, so instead, he'll try to embarrass you by making an example of you in front of your peers. He'll put you to work in the kitchen like a scullery maid."

John grimaced. "Remind me never to be tardy."

JC laughed and slapped him on the back.

"You'll be fine. Just do as you're told and someday you'll be a barrister or maybe a knight like me."

John didn't want to be either, but he didn't want to insult his cousin by saying so. "Since you've become a knight like you wanted, what are your plans now?"

"Next I shall endear myself to the king and become a baron." He raised his glass to a maiden who was watching him from across the room. "The barons get all the young lasses."

John looked over at the girl and thought her homely, far too skinny and with too many freckles to be even slightly attractive. "Well, I don't think you need to become a baron to get all the lasses."

"Don't you enjoy the attention of the ladies?"

John shook his head. "I'd much rather feel the sun and spray on my face and see the froth on top of the waves."

JC patted John on the shoulder. "You'll outgrow that, cousin. Middle Temple will expand your mind, and someday a maiden will come along and make you forget all about the sea. Let's stop talking about school and go chat with some wenches, shall we?"

* * *

A few months later, John reluctantly packed his clothing into a trunk in preparation to move to London and begin his schooling at Middle Temple. Though his heart longed for great adventures, he had never been away from home and harbored trepidations about leaving for the first time. He was thankful Thomas would be accompanying him.

Thomas, on the other hand, was overjoyed by the prospect of spending time in high-minded salons, and he couldn't pack his belongings fast enough. Their stepmother kissed them and made them promise to eat well. Cicely and Frances cried and hugged their brothers. Mrs. Woodbury beamed with pride that her boys were now young men boldly venturing into the world to claim their fortunes. Johannes patted their shoulders and in no uncertain terms reminded them that they were Culpeppers and would not embarrass him by participating in anything foolish. After they boarded the carriage, Thomas chatted for ten full days while they traveled to London. John couldn't wait to get away from the incessant babbling.

The boys arrived two days before classes were to begin and entered Temple Garden through a large archway that was flanked by stone columns. They weaved their way down the path that ran between bushes and trees while white marble statues gazed down upon them. John thought the surroundings looked more like a monastery than an institute of higher learning. At the end of the secluded garden, they entered the serene courtyard with a large fountain in the center. John guessed this to be Fountain Court, which he had heard so much about. So far, this place was nothing more than pretentiousness at its finest. Why would a school need gardens and statues and fountains? The boys passed the rounded stone walls and towering steeple of Temple Church and finally came to a sign in front of a building that read *Temple Hall.* They entered the front door and were instructed by an elderly bearded gentleman to go next door to the admissions office, where they would be assigned their sleeping quarters.

Their rooms were located in the two-story building behind the library. On the way to their rooms, John poked his head in the library and thought it smaller than it should be, considering this was an establishment of higher learning. It was not much larger than the library at his grandfather's estate. John closed the library door and frowned. Being one of the revered inns of higher education in the whole country, Middle Temple should be more impressive.

When John finally located his atrociously small room on the second floor, he was taken aback by the dank and dusty odor. He peeked behind the desk and the wardrobe, searching for a dead mouse. After not finding any demised creatures, he sat down on the edge of the bed and scanned the room.

Three pieces of furniture crowded the room—a desk, a wardrobe, and a lumpy bed. The bed was a wooden frame topped with a small hay-filled mattress. Sharp ends of the hay poked through the worn fabric and scratched his legs. He already missed his comfortable wool-filled mattress at home.

He fell backward and lay flat. At least the bed wasn't sagging in the middle. There was only one small window, situated directly above the desk, and the dreary clouds didn't help with the lighting. He wondered if he should search the other rooms on his floor for a lamp. With only gray stone walls surrounding him and no fireplace, he assumed he would have to leave his door open come winter for the heat to rise from the fireplace in the main gallery. If not, he would surely freeze to death. He sat up and pouted.

That evening and the next, John and Thomas met a few of the boys who lingered in the hallways and on the grounds. There was thick anticipation as the boys became acquainted with their schoolmates and chatted about their coming lessons. Thomas joined in their enthusiasm, discussing literature, law, and their soon-to-be professors. John was polite but quiet. He couldn't care less who his instructor was, as long as it wasn't the wicked Barnaby that JC had warned him about. John was content to remain alone in his room most of the time, while also deeply concerned that sheer boredom would cause his demise. These boys didn't understand he was not a scholar. He was an adventurer, and had no interest in law or literature or making friends with a gaggle of aspiring benchers. John was sure he had taken more than enough language and literature lessons from his tutor over the past eleven years to last him the rest of his life. He wanted nothing more than to run away from this pompous school and hop aboard the nearest ship, but at the age of fifteen, he was required to do as his father instructed. It would be a few more years before he could set sail.

After finding a lamp, he sat down at his small desk with paper and ink. For the next hour, he scribbled out a calendar of the next four years and began crossing off the days before his classes had even begun. He hoped something or someone would come along to help him pass the time, which was surely to move at a snail's pace. After crossing off today on his calendar, he drummed his fingers on his desk and looked around the room. His eyes fell upon his trunk. Perhaps he should unpack.

CHAPTER 10
May 1621,
Middle Temple

Two dozen boys, eager and wide eyed, watched a man enter the room. He wore a long black robe with golden ropes hanging around his neck, ending in knotted tassels at his knees. His long white beard showed him to be of considerable age, resembling someone's grandfather more than the leader of an intellectual community. His aged blue eyes twinkled as he smiled and nodded to the group.

"Good morning, boys. I trust you all found your sleeping chambers adequate. I am Sir Marlowe the Worshipful. I and the other Masters of the Bench warmly welcome you to the Honorable Society of the Middle Temple." He began pacing back and forth with his fingers entwined behind his back. "For the next few years, you will immerse yourselves in literature and law. You will study day and night, and you will complete your lessons on time and in full. I trust you will mind your behavior and conduct yourselves accordingly." He stopped pacing when he reached the middle of the room, and turned to the boys. "Eventually, some of you will become apprentices for our esteemed panel of barristers and lawyers, or you may take the role of clerk. Some of you may even elevate to the role of sheriff. A very few of you may find yourself as a bencher or serve in Parliament. There is a very slim possibility you'd even be called to the king's service as a knight. I wish you all a successful academia and trust you will embrace every opportunity that lies before you."

Another man also wearing a black robe and golden ropes stood in the doorway and cleared his throat. The speaker looked over his shoulder at the man, then turned back to the pupils. "And now, I'd like to introduce you to your illustrious headmaster, Sidney Barnaby."

John grimaced, but he and Thomas clapped along with the other boys as the headmaster strolled toward the center of the room. The man looked as stern as JC had warned. A pair of spectacles rested on the tip of his pointed nose, and his rather large ears stuck out from under his cap. He began stroking his goatee as if caressing the family pet. For a moment, John couldn't put his finger on what was so amusing about the man's appearance, then it struck him—the man looked like a goat. John tried unsuccessfully to stifle a giggle.

Barnaby's brow wrinkled and the corners of this mouth turned down like a fish as he scanned the group of boys. He looked at each one as if viewing a repulsive heap of trash. He cleared his throat and his Adam's apple bobbed up and down. Just as he opened his mouth to speak, a frizzy-headed boy ran into the room, allowing the door to slam behind him. The sound echoed loudly within the stone walls and the tardy boy's face turned red with embarrassment. Barnaby followed the boy's movement with his narrowed eyes as the boy took the only empty seat in the room—right next to John. John felt a trickle of sweat drip down his back as the headmaster slowly walked toward them.

"You're tardy for my class," the man scoffed, his eyes filled with hostility. When he said the word class, he drew out the a for an inappropriate amount of time, and John was again reminded of a goat, but with the man standing directly in front of him, he didn't dare giggle.

"My apologies. I just arrived, sir."

"What is your name, boy?" Barnaby growled.

"William Berkeley, sir."

"William Berkeley." He stared at Berkeley for a long time, as if attempting to memorize every feature of the boy's face. He then repeated the name. After what seemed like an hour of uncomfortable silence, with the tension in the room growing by the second, Barnaby said, "William Berkeley, I will speak with you in private following this evening's supper."

"Yes, sir." William lowered his eyes to the floor.

As Barnaby turned his back on Berkeley and returned to the center of the room, Berkeley glanced around the room at the other boys. John wondered if Berkeley's humility was in respect for the headmaster or due to his embarrassment for being late, or both.

Berkeley leaned over to John and whispered, "Who's *that* old goat?"

John almost laughed out loud and his hands flew up to his mouth.

Berkeley winked at him and grinned.

John knew then that Berkeley's reaction was

neither out of respect nor embarrassment. It was a game Berkeley liked to play. John was pleased to finally find someone at this school he could be friends with.

Over Berkeley's shoulder, John saw Thomas frown and shake his head at his little brother. John composed himself and brought his attention to the headmaster.

Barnaby sneered at the assembly before finally beginning his nasally diatribe. "Under my tutelage, you will learn the disciplines of arguing, ethical sensibilities, legal concepts, and interpretation. The most important thing you will learn is that you will be timely for all of my classes." He paused and gazed over the rim of his glasses at Berkeley for such a long moment that the entire room grew uneasy again.

Even though John found Barnaby's appearance comical, the man certainly had a way of making a group of people feel anxious. John decided to study this technique. It might come in handy someday when commanding a ship full of sailors.

Barnaby cleared his throat again. "Gentlemen, you will become skilled at narrative and rhetoric, as well as the art of persuasion. When you are not studying under my supervision, you will be educated in the arts of fencing, acting, and writing. During your free time, which will be quite infrequent, you will eat, study, and work together. I will not tolerate any foolishness from any of you or you will be expelled. And you, William Berkeley, are the first on my list to keep my eye on."

Barnaby pointed to John. "What is your name, boy?"

John sat up straight. "John Culpepper, sir."

"John Culpepper, huh? Son of Johannes?"

"Yes, sir."

"Related to JC?"

"Yes, sir. He's my cousin."

"I heard JC was knighted."

"Yes, sir, he was."

"Well, since you're a Culpepper, and typically Culpeppers like to take charge, your first duty as a scholar of Middle Temple is to take Mr. Berkeley to the Office of Admissions and find his room. I expect both of you to be on time for your lesson, which begins promptly in ten minutes in the library."

"Yes, sir." John nodded.

Barnaby turned to the group. "Everyone is dismissed." He walked toward the podium and looked down at it as if he had forgotten anyone else was in the room.

All of the boys simultaneously rose from the benches, and the clamor grew as they ambled from the room. "Quietly," Barnaby shouted. Each student passed through Barnaby's scrutiny on his way out.

When Thomas, John, and William reached the fresh air of the courtyard, John stopped and turned to Berkeley. "I'm John Culpepper and this is my brother Thomas."

"It's a pleasure to make your acquaintance. My friends and family call me Will. I'm sorry I arrived late and got you involved."

"Oh, nonsense. It's good to start the year off with a little fun, especially with a headmaster like Barnaby. We'll have to put our heads together and come up with some good pranks to pull on him."

Thomas shook his head.

"Thomas, the man looks like a *goat*!" John screeched.

Will laughed.

Thomas rolled his eyes but John ignored him as he continued, "For now, let's hurry to the office and find your sleeping chambers, Will."

When they arrived at the office, the clerk didn't have any trouble locating Will's room. Apparently Berkeley was the only pupil who had not checked in yet and the men in the office had been discussing his tardiness. "Your room is in the building behind the library, the second floor, room 200."

"That's great!" exclaimed John.

"What's great?" asked Will.

"That's the room next to mine!"

CHAPTER 11
A Few Days Later

John lay on his bed, arms folded behind his head and ankles crossed. He stared at a spider walking on the ceiling and admired its ability to walk upside down without falling. He heard a rap on his door, immediately followed by Thomas entering.

"What are you doing?" Thomas asked him.

"Nothing."

"Is something wrong?"

"No, nothing's wrong. I'm just bored. I'd rather go home."

"You'd rather go home? But I thought you wanted to be an adventurer, sail the world, experience exciting things."

"You call this exciting? I can think of a lot of things more exciting than lying here watching a spider walk across my ceiling and attending boring classes with our goat—I mean, instructor—every day."

"Oh, leave Barnaby alone. You know, Middle Temple has abundant opportunities if you'd simply give it a chance."

"Thomas, you love books and studies so I'm sure you're happy here, but I could just die." He pulled the pillow from behind his head and covered his face with it.

Thomas grabbed the pillow. "Stop being so dramatic."

John sat up on the bed, his face suddenly filled with excitement. He swung his legs over the side of the bed. "I'm thinking up some pranks for the old goat."

"Little brother, I think you should focus on your studies instead of inventing ways to drive Barnaby crazy."

"He's already crazy." John grabbed his pillow back from Thomas and tossed it on the bed.

Thomas shook his head. "Anyway, I came by to offer you a remedy for your boredom. Since we don't have class until late this evening, let's go up the road and have supper at the inn. I'm sick of eating at the hall, and some of the other boys said Ye Olde Clock Tavern has pretty good food."

John shrugged. "Sure. Do you want to invite Will?"

"Of course. You go find him and I'll go get my hat. I'll meet you downstairs."

The three boys walked past the gatehouse bordering Temple grounds and turned right when they reached the river. They had followed the dry dirt road for nearly a mile when they came across the small inn. The outside was old and gloomy and they entered to the smell of ale and piss. They glanced at each other in doubt.

When their eyes adjusted to the dimness of the room, they noticed a few of the patrons were old drunkards, but most were scholars from Middle Temple. The boys found an empty table in the corner. Thomas wiped crumbs off the chair before he sat down. John didn't seem to notice the filth.

"I hope they cook better than they clean," Thomas said, wiping his palm on his shirt.

Will pursed his lips. John wrinkled his nose and shrugged.

"Are you sure you want to eat here?" asked Will.

"Everyone says they have good food, and a lot of our fellow students are here, so…" Thomas said.

John had been scanning the room and noticed a boy sitting alone at a table in the opposite corner. He recognized the lad from class and gestured to Thomas that he was going to talk to the loner. "Order whatever they have for me. I'll be right back."

John returned a few minutes later with the redheaded boy in tow.

"Thomas, Will, I'd like you to meet Jasper Churchyard. Jasper, this is Will Berkeley and my brother Thomas Culpepper."

Jasper shyly nodded at the boys and possibly said hello, but it wasn't much more than a murmur. Will invited him to join them. Jasper placed his books on the table and sat down. He sat on the edge of the chair, looking as if he might need to make a hurried escape.

"So, Jasper, where are you from?" Thomas asked.

"London." The boy spoke barely louder than a whisper.

Will laughed. "People other than maids and paupers actually live in London?"

Jasper nodded. "My father is a poet and he says sages and muses surround us in the city. They help him write." He shrugged.

"Well, that sounds interesting, Jasper," John said. He narrowed his eyes at Will and Thomas, warning them to be gentlemanly. "What do you think of Barnaby?"

"He's all right."

"Really? He reminds me of a goat." John laughed.

Jasper smiled. "Yes, now that you mention it, he does resemble a goat."

"Where do you stay at Middle Temple?" John asked.

"In the building behind the library. It's the same room my father had when he attended."

"Really? Our father attended here also." He gestured to Thomas. "We're also in that building. Will is in 200, I'm next door, and Thomas is across the hall."

"I'm in 210."

The boys ordered mutton and ale and Jasper finally relaxed and sat on the whole chair. They drank and talked for hours, gossiping about other students and making jokes about their headmaster. When John began imitating Barnaby, complete with extending the a sound of every word, their laughter wouldn't subside. Will and John were both wiping tears from their eyes when they heard the Temple Church bells chime.

"What time is it?" Jasper asked with panic in his voice.

The boys sat silent. The bells rang seven times and stopped.

Barnaby's evening class began at seven o'clock, but they had lost track of time. They all jumped up and ran to the door.

CHAPTER 12
Headmaster Barnaby

The four boys ran all the way back to the school and were panting heavily when they passed through the Temple gatehouse. The man in the window asked, "Aren't you boys late for class?"

They didn't answer him and kept running. When they reached the library door, they were too frightened to enter.

"Do you think we'll get into trouble if we enter late?" asked Jasper.

The other three boys looked at him as if he had just asked if the grass was green.

After a few minutes of negotiations, they decided to skip the class and not subject themselves to the humiliation of entering late. Hopefully Barnaby wouldn't notice their absence.

Unfortunately, Barnaby did notice. The next morning at their eight o'clock class, he was ready for them. After the class was seated and quiet, Barnaby paced the stone floor, loudly slapping a thin piece of wood against his palm. Each click of his heels on the floor echoed around the room.

"We seem to have a serious truancy problem

in my class."

John and Will glanced at each other and grinned when Barnaby drew out the a in class.

Barnaby paused his pacing and looked around the room, his gaze resting momentarily on various students. John looked at Jasper and saw a bead of sweat resting on the boy's forehead. Jasper was staring at the floor and didn't even look like he was breathing. John wanted to ease Jasper's fear but couldn't get his friend's attention to smile at him. Whatever happened, they were all in this together. It would be all right.

"There are some young men here who think it's more important to loiter at the inn and drink ale than it is to attend their lesson."

John watched Barnaby resume his pacing and wondered how the old goat knew where they had been. The tension in the room grew as the entire class nervously watched and waited. Finally, Barnaby stopped in front of Will and spun to face him. "William Berkeley!" he snapped.

Will stood up. "Yes, sir."

"This is your second offense and it will therefore be noted in your records. You will meet me after this class to discuss your truancy and your punishment. There is a great probability that you will be expelled for your disruptive behavior immediately following your next offense, which I can say with great confidence will come very soon." He stood no more than a couple inches from Will's face. John imagined Will could smell the old goat's rancid breath. "I hope you are aware that I have no qualms whatsoever in dismissing you from Middle Temple. This is an institution for exemplary scholastic achievement, not for impertinent conduct."

Will remained still.

"Be seated," Barnaby barked.

Will sat.

Barnaby scanned the room and eventually his gaze fell upon John. At that precise moment, John and Will were smiling at each other ever so slightly.

"John Culpepper!"

John jumped to his feet. "Yes, sir."

"Is there something humorous that I am missing?"

"No, sir."

Barnaby walked toward John, slowly shaking his head. "I am highly disappointed in you. Your name alone holds great promise, but obviously every family has its black sheep."

John narrowed his eyes at Barnaby, anger building. How dare this pompous ass denounce the Culpepper name? What kind of name was Barnaby? What land and title did his family hold? He was nothing more than a troll playing the role of a tyrant, an oppressor with the single talent of boring his students to death with his tedious lessons, a big-eared mule with the voice of a billy goat who was unknowingly the court jester of the entire school. John didn't need to attend classes on rhetoric and arguing. He had plenty to say to this man right now.

"Is there something you would like to say, John?"

Thomas tapped John on the back of his leg and under his breath said, "Stop."

John paused, knowing his brother was right. If he opened his mouth right now, he would surely be expelled. And if one thought Barnaby's consequences were severe, one had never experienced the wrath of Johannes Culpepper. John clenched his jaw and shook his head. "Nothing, sir."

"Very good. This is your first offense and I trust there will be no further incidents."

"Yes, sir."

"Be seated."

John sat.

Barnaby looked at Thomas. "And the same goes for you, Thomas Culpepper."

Thomas rose, muttered, "Yes, sir," and sat back down.

Will and John glanced at each other again. Apparently Barnaby had a sliver of respect for the Culpepper name, or at least for the Culpepper money, and had taken a liking to Thomas and would not embarrass him in front of the group. That fact made Will and John disrespect the old goat even more. They watched Barnaby walk toward his lectern, hoping the tongue-lashing was over.

"Jasper Churchyard!" Barnaby bellowed and the whole class jumped.

Jasper slowly rose to his feet, jaw tense, and eyes to the floor. His hands were clasped in front of him and his shoulders hunched. He trembled and looked so pale, John thought the boy may faint at any moment.

"Stand up straight!" Barnaby slapped his stick on his lectern, causing everyone in the room to jump again. He left the stick lying on the lectern as he clasped his hands behind his back and strolled toward Jasper. He cleared his throat, a sure sign he was going to speak for a considerable length of time. "Young man, were the rules not explained to you when you entered Middle Temple?"

"They were, sir," Jasper mumbled.

"Did you not understand them?"

"I understood them, sir."

"Then why do you choose to ignore them?"

"It was a mistake, sir. It won't happen again."

Barnaby stopped in front of Jasper, his pointed nose only inches from Jasper's face. "It unquestionably was a mistake, and it certainly won't happen again. You see, I don't need to tolerate truancy from you, as your father doesn't care whether you attend here or not. He probably doesn't even know where you are at this moment, does he? As a matter of fact, I can expel you right now and not one person at Middle Temple or in the entire city of London would care. Isn't that right, Mr. Churchyard?"

"Yes, sir," Jasper murmured, his eyes filling with tears.

"I'm sorry, I didn't hear you. Speak up so the entire class can understand your drivel. You don't have a father who cares whether you graduate from Middle Temple or not. Isn't that correct?"

"That's correct, sir." A tear rolled down Jasper's cheek.

"Your father attended school here, did he not?"

Jasper nodded.

"But he couldn't handle the rigors of law studies, either, isn't that correct?"

Jasper nodded again. A second tear rolled.

"Your father dropped out of my class because it was too challenging for him. He would rather avail his time writing poetry and verse. Such a frivolous pursuit." He paused, but Jasper said nothing. Barnaby leaned his chin down and looked over the rim of his glasses at Jasper. The tension in the room grew to the thickness of day-old porridge. Finally Barnaby said, "Jasper Churchyard, the punishment for your truancy will be thirty nights' work in the kitchen. Beginning this evening, following our supper, you will clean the entire kitchen by yourself. You will not be late again."

Jasper nodded and sat down, sniffling and wiping the tears from his cheeks with the back of his hand.

John felt rage boiling in his chest and knew his cheeks were red with anger. Thomas nudged John's foot and shook his head ever so slightly. John bit the inside of his cheek and exhaled loudly through his nose. He would stay composed for now, but someday very soon, Barnaby would get his.

Every night for the next four weeks, John slipped across Temple Garden and into the kitchen to help Jasper clean. By the time they finished washing dishes and pots and pans, cleaning out the hearth, mopping the floor, and restocking the pantry, time had crept into the wee hours of the morning. If Jasper had to do all the work alone, he would never have finished before the women arrived to prepare breakfast.

"Thank you for helping me, John. If this was solitary labor, I'd be in even more trouble for not finishing the task."

"That's what friends are for. And it gives me something to do besides sit around Fountain Court and listen to the poetry students babble on. I can't stand hearing their drivel about their lost loves and fair maidens. Makes me sick."

"That's the kind of verse my father writes, too."

"My darling maiden fair, blah blah blah. They should write verses about Barnaby. That would be more entertaining. My precious goaty goat, bah bah baaah."

They both laughed.

John lifted a stack of clean plates, placed them on the shelf, and turned to Jasper. "You know what we should do? We should spend these hours deciding how to get Barnaby back."

"What do you mean, get him back?"

"You know, we'll play a prank on him. Serves him right for picking on you."

"I don't know, John. I don't want to get into any more trouble."

"The only way you get into trouble is if you get caught, so we'll come up with something so clever, we'll never get caught."

"Well, all right. What shall we do?"

John thought about it for a minute as he dried the iron pot Jasper had just washed.

"I know!" John stopped drying the pot and shook his damp rag toward Jasper. "You know how we're always saying Barnaby looks and sounds like a goat? Let's find a real goat and dress him in black robes and picket him in the middle of Temple Garden!"

A grin came to Jasper's face. "John, you have such an evil mind. Where can we get a goat?"

"Don't you worry about it. I'll find one within the next few weeks and everyone will get a big laugh out of Goaty Barnaby munching on grass in the garden."

The boys worked quietly for the next hour while John racked his brain for ideas to design a costume for the goat. He knew he had an old black cloak he could transform into a cape, so he only needed to find some gold-colored rope to hang around the goat's neck.

Jasper broke the silence. "What do you want to do when you graduate from Middle Temple?"

"I don't want to do anything that has to do with law. I'm only here because my father is a lawyer and wants me to follow in his footsteps. He demands that I attend. What I really want to do is buy a ship and sail the seas."

"A ship? What does your father say about that?"

"He threatened to disown me."

"He sounds tough."

"Tough is a mild word when describing my father, but it's all right. I don't need his lands or money to sail a ship. I'll sleep beneath the stars on the open decks and feed off fresh fish from the ocean. I shall ride the currents with the wind at my back, scampering up the ropes to the highest mast to tighten the sails."

"That sounds grand. Where would you like to sail?"

"Maybe the Orient or the new colonies."

After a moment, Jasper said, "I think I shall like to sail with you, John."

"It's done, then. You shall be my quartermaster! But first, we need to find a goat."

* * *

The four boys were studying in the library a few weeks later when Johannes Culpepper stomped in through the archway of the library door. His heavy boots echoed off the stone floor and paneled walls and disturbed the quiet room, causing every student to look up from their studies. Johannes's sheer size was daunting, and in his broad-shouldered jerkin with his large hat, he looked even more intimidating. His face was red and his eyes were narrowed. His jaw twitched in anger. He marched straight to the table in the center of the room where John, Thomas, and their friends sat.

Thomas looked up in surprise. "Father! What brings you here?"

"I've gotten word in London that someone is misbehaving." He glared across the table at John.

"No, Father, that's not true," countered John.

"We will discuss this outside. Both of you, come with me." He marched out the back door and into Temple Garden with John and Thomas trailing close behind. By the time they reached the middle of the yard, faces of schoolboys had pressed against the diamond-shaped panes of glass, watching and listening for the heated argument that was surely to begin.

Johannes stood with his hands on his hips, chastising the boys about something, but the students inside the library couldn't make out what he was saying. Johannes's face was red and veins bulged from his temples, but John didn't look angry. As a matter of fact, he looked quite amused.

John and Thomas faced their father, and directly behind him, picketed in the middle of the garden, was a white goat, dressed in a black robe with gold cords around its neck. Next to the goat stood Barnaby, his hands on his hips, his face purple with anger as he glared at the goat. The goat looked up at Barnaby and let out a loud "baaaa!" John couldn't stifle his laughter. He turned away from his father and pretended to have a coughing fit.

The students in the library erupted in laughter as well. John bit his lip in an effort to stop laughing and turned back toward his father.

"John, are you listening to me?"

"Yes, Father, I am."

"Why do I hear you are not attending your classes? Why are you making your headmaster angry?"

"Me?! What about Thomas? I never missed a class when he wasn't right there with me."

Johannes backhanded John across the face with such force it almost knocked him to the ground. "Do not raise your voice to me, boy!"

John rubbed his cheek and glared at his father. He instantly became aware of his action and quickly looked down at the ground. He stretched open his mouth to ease the pain in his jaw and blinked a few times to erase the stars he was seeing.

"Thomas, is this true?"

"Yes, Father."

"Then why am I only getting word of John misbehaving?"

"I don't know, Father. Headmaster Barnaby doesn't seem to like John very much."

"Then I shall have a conversation with Barnaby and find out the reason."

Thomas pointed over Johannes's shoulder.

"He's right there. Perhaps you should speak with him now."

Johannes turned and marched across the grass.

"Are you all right?" Thomas asked John.

John nodded as he rubbed his cheek.

"Tell me you had nothing to do with that goat," Thomas whispered.

John still couldn't answer. If he opened his mouth even a little bit, laughter would escape.

"Let's go back inside," Thomas said. He and John hurried back toward the library. When they entered, they saw most of the boys crowded around the windows, howling at the sight of the goat. The boys were asking one another where it could have possibly come from. None of them noticed John and Thomas entering the room.

"Is everything all right?" whispered Jasper across the table after John sat down.

John nodded. "Did you look outside?"

"No, I was afraid to see what was going to happen. Is your father angry?"

John picked up his quill and opened his book. "Don't worry about my father. Go take a look out the window."

Jasper walked over to the window. He pushed his way through the throng of boys who were blocking his view. After he looked out the window, he turned back and looked at John with a huge grin on his face.

John nodded and smiled.

Thomas looked across the table at his brother. "John, tell me where the goat came from."

"I have no idea."

CHAPTER 13
Spring 1623,
Middle Temple

Just as Thomas had done nearly every day for the last two years, he rapped on John's bedroom door and entered without an invitation. Although the sun had risen hours ago, John was curled up in a ball, facing the wall, still asleep. Thomas tapped him on the back.

"John, wake up. I have exciting news!"

"What is it?" John mumbled as he rolled over onto his back. He didn't open his eyes.

"Are you awake? This is important."

"What can be so important that you have to wake me up on a Saturday morning?"

Thomas rattled a piece of paper in John's face. "Read this!"

John sat up, rubbed his eyes, and groggily took the paper from Thomas. After a few moments, he looked back up. "Is this true?"

"Yes, little brother. I am now a member of the Virginia Company. Our kinsman, George Scott, died and passed shares on to me."

"Who is George Scott?"

"Uncle Alexander's father-in-law. He left three shares to his grandson Warham and three shares to me."

"Why would he leave you shares?"

"Since Uncle Alexander doesn't have any children of his own, and I'm his eldest nephew, I guess I'm next in line." He shrugged. "But it makes me wonder about something I heard last Yuletide."

"What did you hear? What are you talking about?"

"The last time we were home, I overheard Father and Uncle Alexander talking about Katherine St. Leger, and that she and I would be a good match. I didn't understand it at the time, but now with this endowment, I wonder if they're trying to coax me out to Leeds Castle and see her."

"Katherine, our little cousin?"

"Well, she's not little anymore. She's my age. And she's not actually our cousin. Uncle Alexander married widow Mary St. Ledger, and Katherine is her granddaughter. She's Warham St. Ledger's daughter. Since he's always at sea, Uncle Alexander raised Katherine. Don't you remember playing with her at Grandfather's house when we were small?"

"Yes, of course, but what does all this have to do with you and the Virginia Company?"

"I'm not sure. Maybe they're trying to find her a husband."

John kicked off his blanket and hung his bare legs over the side of the bed. "A husband? I can't imagine you being some silly girl's husband."

"Well, nevertheless, I'm going to travel to Leeds Castle to thank them and to visit with Uncle Alexander."

There were so many things running through John's mind, he didn't know where to start, and none of them had anything to do with Katherine St. Leger. His first thought was wondering if Thomas would now finance sailings to the Virginia Colony. This created a whole new range of possibilities for John's future. The second thought was that he would like to accompany Thomas to Leeds Castle, but not to see Uncle Alexander. He would like to speak with Warham St. Leger. He wanted to hear stories of Warham's adventures and ask him how to go about buying his own ship. John didn't know if Warham was at Leeds Castle or at sea. He would have to find out.

He waved the piece of paper toward Thomas. "What exactly does this mean for you, Thomas?"

"It means I shall make money as a shareholder in the Virginia Company and future expeditions will be for my benefit." Thomas's eyes lit up in excitement. "It means I have begun to amass my own wealth, and once we graduate from Middle Temple, I shall be on my way to becoming a true country gentleman like our father."

John frowned. "I don't know why you'd aspire to that. I could go right back to sleep if I imagine how grand it would be to live in the country and stare at the same trees for the rest of my life." John dramatically fell back onto his pillow.

* * *

As word of Thomas's endowment spread throughout Middle Temple, other students began to treat him with more respect. He was invited to more events and gatherings, not only by the student body, but also by the men of the upper chambers. He dined with lawyers and debated policy with members of Parliament. He was never at want for companionship around the inn. The boys, sensing Thomas's newfound importance, seemed to flock to him like rats on a good meal of oxen. Even Headmaster Barnaby showed him more respect, and in typical fashion, never missed an opportunity to rub Thomas's fortune in John's face.

One afternoon, John was on his way to the library, staring down at the path as he hustled through Fountain Court. Suddenly there were feet where he was going to step. He stopped abruptly, looked up, and found he was only inches away from the squinting eyes of Headmaster Barnaby. The old goat remained frozen directly in John's path.

"So, I hear your brother is someone important now. That's typical for a Culpepper. Most Culpeppers, anyway. What about you? Why didn't you get any shares in the Virginia Company?" Barnaby asked.

"That's none of your business."

"Mind your tone, young man. You still have two more years under my tutelage, and I can still see to it that you're expelled long before you complete them. You can go right back home with your tail between your legs. What will your father say when you don't receive an apprenticeship?"

"What makes you think I want one? Why would I want anything from this school or from you?"

Barnaby snickered. "Well, I see you have learned to speak your mind and not stare at the floor like a child. Apparently this school has done something positive for you."

"Yes, it has, Headmaster. It has taught me that I don't need to tolerate haughty and arrogant individuals who enjoy nothing more than bullying those they are supposed to be protecting and teaching."

Students who were studying and conversing around the courtyard silenced. Even the little birds in the hedges quieted their song. The only sound in the courtyard was the faint splashing of water in the fountain as John glared at Barnaby. Barnaby glanced around the courtyard, and when he noticed eavesdroppers on their conversation, his face flushed three shades of red. John didn't know if the colors were caused by anger or embarrassment, and he didn't care. He would be out of Middle Temple soon enough, away from this tyrant. He would find a way to purchase his ship and sail the ocean, and he certainly didn't need Barnaby to do that.

CHAPTER 14
Summer 1623,
Leeds Castle

The following summer, Thomas and John separated for the first time in their lives. John returned home to Astwood Court, and Thomas rode out to Leeds Castle to visit Uncle Alexander. Even though Leeds Castle was only a couple hours' ride from Middle Temple, the boys had never ventured out there, and Thomas hadn't seen his uncle since his summers at Wigsell Manor when he was just a boy.

His initial impression of the castle was one of awe. From the distance, its white stone walls and square turrets loomed above the green countryside like a phoenix rising from the ashes. As he drew closer, he saw it was a motte-and-bailey castle, a house sitting on a raised earthwork in the middle of water. His father's house sat in the middle of a moat the size of a small river, but this house was surrounded by a body of water the size of a lake. Black swans floated among white and pink water lilies. Herons and plovers tiptoed around the marshy edges, picking for insects between the stalks of cat 'o nine tails. Clusters of yellow flowers grew around the castle walls, painting bright splatters on the white stone.

Thomas pulled his horse to a stop so he could take in the beauty of the dwelling. It was like a painting. After a few moments, he inched his horse forward, and the closer he got to the castle, the grander it became. It was larger than Middle Temple, Astwood Court, and Wigsell Manor combined. He neared the drawbridge and stopped to see if anyone would come out and greet him, but no one did. He decided to cross the drawbridge, but his horse didn't think well of the idea. He had to force the animal to step onto the wooden planks and kept a tight hold on the reins so the beast wouldn't turn around and sprint. They were both relieved when the horse stepped off the bridge on the other side and onto the dirt again.

Thomas nearly didn't recognize the man who appeared in the courtyard, emerging from an arched doorway.

"Nephew! I'm glad you've arrived."

This was certainly not the man Thomas knew as his uncle nearly fifteen years ago. This was a fifty-year-old vagabond with gray hair and wrinkles around his eyes. His clothes were tattered, his knees covered with mud, his face smeared with soot. The last time Thomas saw his uncle, Alexander had been in the prime of his life. Now, he looked like a beggar.

"Uncle?" Thomas asked.

"Yes, boy." Alexander took the horse's halter. "Hop down. Let me get a look at you."

Thomas climbed down. Alexander shook his

hand and gave him a hug.

"You'll have to excuse my appearance. I was working in the garden, and then I offered to help my servant sweep the chimneys. I'm afraid I must look a mess."

Thomas laughed. "Well, I was thinking you look a bit like a vagrant."

"Yes, I suppose I do."

Alexander called for a servant who appeared from around the corner and took Thomas's horse. "Come into the house and we'll get you something cool to drink." Thomas followed him through the doorway. "I'll get myself cleaned up."

Thomas sat alone in one of the reception rooms, admiring the grandness of the estate. Tapestries and paintings adorned the oak-paneled walls. Marble statues watched him from nearly every corner. The ornately carved woodwork on the beamed ceilings held the most exquisite impressions Thomas had ever seen. A pendulum clock ticked from the mantel. Thomas was drawn to a portrait on the wall behind it. A young lady with auburn curls sat regally next to two large brown-and-white hunting dogs. Her green eyes almost jumped off the canvas. He wondered if the painting was his uncle's wife in her earlier years. As he admired it, Uncle Alexander entered.

"There! I'm cleaned up and ready to greet you now."

Thomas was surprised by the transformation. His uncle was dressed in breeches with tall boots turned over at the top, and covering his linen shirt was a doublet with paneled sleeves. He looked like the Sir Alexander Culpepper everyone knew and respected, and Thomas was rightfully impressed.

The two moved into the dining room, where they supped on minced pies, sipped wine, and chatted about school and the family. They were discussing Johannes and Astwood Court as the evening sun began its descent and peeked through the stained-glass windows in the entryway. The light bounced off the tile floor and lit the dining room doorway as if the sun was shining directly into it. When a shadow appeared, Thomas looked toward the doorway and saw a graceful silhouette. The woman it belonged to floated into the room like an angel in an emerald gown, her auburn curls dancing on her shoulders with each step. It was the woman from the painting. This was not his uncle's wife. This maiden was much too young.

Thomas stared at her. He was sure his uncle was still speaking, but he couldn't make out what the man was saying. His uncle's voice sounded as if it were a mountain and valley away. She stepped into the room and Thomas felt as if he couldn't catch his next breath. He couldn't take his eyes off her. Everything else in the room disappeared. The woman in front of him was even more beautiful than in the painting, and when she grinned and waved her fingers at him, he recognized her smile. It was Katherine, whom he hadn't seen since they were children. Those days spent at his grandfather's house seemed a million years ago. The last time he saw Katherine, they couldn't have been more than nine or ten years old. His uncle turned to see what Thomas was looking at.

"Oh, Thomas, you remember my granddaughter, Katherine, don't you?" Alexander said as he rose to greet her.

Thomas also stood to greet her. "I certainly do, but we were just children the last time we saw each other." He certainly didn't remember her being so beautiful. He also didn't remember getting butterflies in his stomach. She kissed Alexander on the cheek and turned her attention to Thomas. As she walked closer, her hand outstretched to meet his, he saw the lightest freckles adorning the bridge of her nose.

"Thomas, it's so nice to see you again after all these years," she said as she allowed him to take her hand.

"And you, Katherine. I must say you have grown into a lovely woman." Her skin was like alabaster. He stared into her eyes as he kissed her fingers.

"Thank you very much." She beamed. "I was going to sit on the terrace to enjoy the last of the day's sunshine. Would you gentlemen care to join me?"

"You two go on ahead and catch up. I have some work to do," Alexander said.

"Thomas?" she asked.

He nodded, uncharacteristically speechless. She held out her elbow for him to escort her.

"I'll speak with you two later at supper," Alexander said as they exited the room.

"Certainly, Uncle," Thomas mumbled, distracted.

Katherine led Thomas through the hallway to the back of the house, where they sat on the terrace and spent the afternoon becoming reacquainted.

By the end of the day, Thomas knew this

woman would be his wife.

CHAPTER 15
Yuletide 1623,
Astwood Court

Johannes tapped his knife on his crystal wine goblet to get the family's attention. When the group quieted down, he raised his glass high. "I'd like to wish you all a happy Yuletide and tell you all how happy I am to spend the season with you."

They all raised their glasses.

"Happy Yuletide to you, husband," Eleanor smiled.

"Yes, Father, happy Yuletide," Thomas chimed in.

Johannes continued. "I'd also like to take a moment to acknowledge Thomas's successes and achievements. As you all know, he was given three shares of the Virginia Company by George Scott, and we have recently learned that he has also been offered an apprenticeship with my cousin Sir Thomas Culpepper, who serves in Parliament and has chambers at Middle Temple." He looked at Thomas. "You're going to have a struggle keeping people from confusing the two of you, but if anyone takes you for him, you should be greatly honored, for Sir Thomas is a well-respected member of court. You will learn much from him." He raised his glass. "Son, we are all very proud of your accomplishments and wish you much success in the future."

"Cheers!" The family raised its glasses.

"I have one more announcement, if you'll all indulge me for a moment," Johannes said as he rose from his chair.

Mrs. Woodbury waddled into the room and stood next to Johannes. He took her hand. Though she still oversaw the girls' daily care as their governess, Eleanor was the one who spent the most time with them, instructing them in all manners of household care, including sewing and weaving, and instructions in music, teaching both girls to play numerous musical instruments and to sing. Frances was quite the gifted vocalist and entertained the family on many occasions, always happy to be the center of attention. Cicely had become a respectable seamstress. She possessed great patience and an eye for detail, and her tapestries and quilts decorated every room at Astwood Court, as well as some of the surrounding homes in Worcestershire.

Through the years, Mrs. Woodbury always conveyed a loving and exuberant personality. On this day she looked tearful.

"I would like to thank Mrs. Woodbury for her twenty-two years of faithful service to our family. Since all of you children are grown now, she has decided to retire to London."

John placed his glass down on the table. He watched a tear work its way down the wrinkles of Mrs. Woodbury's face as her mouth distorted in an attempt to smile. She started to say something, but the words wouldn't form in her mouth. She placed her hand on her chest and looked at the ceiling for a moment, trying to compose herself.

"I thank you from the bottom of my heart for all these years of happiness, m'lord." She looked at each face around the table. "And my beautiful children, thank you for being you. You are all so special to me and I will never forget you. Frances and Cicely, you have both grown into beautiful young women. Thomas and John, I can't tell you how proud I am of the men you've become."

Frances and Cicely jumped up from their chairs and ran to hug her. As she held them in her embrace, Thomas and John rose to hug her also. They towered over her short, round frame as they kissed her on her cheeks. Eleanor finally rose from her seat, walked around the table toward her, and took Mrs. Woodbury's hands in her own.

"Mrs. Woodbury, I don't know what I would have done without you all these years. Entering a marriage with four children could have been extremely difficult, but you made the transition very easy for me. We will miss your presence in the house, and we hope that you will come visit us often," Eleanor said.

"Yes," agreed Johannes. "You are welcome to visit anytime. It won't be the same around here without you."

Mrs. Woodbury nodded. "I would like that very much, m'lord. Thank you...for everything." She placed her hand on her chest and took a deep breath. "Now if you'll all excuse me, I need to finish packing." She exited the room and a somber silence fell.

JC said, "She will be very happy in London. I shall take her there myself and see to it that she is settled into her new flat."

"That would be very kind of you, JC," Eleanor said. She returned to her seat and placed her napkin back on her lap. "Mary, have you ever been to London?"

Mary was Eleanor's seventeen-year-old niece who had recently been orphaned and had come up from Sussex to stay with the family. She was a dark-haired, slender beauty, very shy and conservative, but with a sparkle in her dark brown eyes.

John watched the girl across the table as she shook her head, her hair resting on the shoulders of her scarlet dress.

"No, Aunt Eleanor, I've never been to London." Her voice was like smooth silk.

"Not at all? Ever?" John asked.

"I'm afraid not." Mary blushed. "My father was partial to life in the country and never took us into town."

Thomas spoke up. "Well, then, you'll have to come and visit us at Middle Temple."

"Yes, please come and visit," John added. "We will show you all around. It's quite an amazing place."

"I would like that very much. Thank you," she said, looking back down at her plate.

John picked up his goblet and took a deep drink of wine, watching Mary over the rim.

She glanced up at him, and just as quickly diverted her eyes back to her plate. When she raised her eyes again, John was still watching her from across the table.

* * *

As the Yuletide season came to a close, Mrs. Woodbury's belongings were loaded into JC's coach, and the family joined them outside to say their tearful good-byes. Eleanor didn't take part in the farewell, as she had taken ill the morning following the Yuletide feast. She hadn't come down from her room for the last five days, and her chamber servant said she hadn't gotten out of bed even once during that time. Eleanor was racked with fever and stomach pain, and the entire family was very concerned, especially Thomas.

"Father, do you think we should stay until Eleanor feels better?" he asked.

Johannes rubbed his gray beard as he looked out the office window at the snowy landscape below. "I know you need to get back to your studies and your work. That's imperative."

"Yes, I know it is, but what if Eleanor takes a long time to convalesce?"

Johannes looked down at the floor. "The doctor came to see her early this morning. He said there's nothing he can do for her. He said to prepare ourselves."

"What? He doesn't think she's going to improve?"

Johannes shook his head and returned his gaze to the horizon.

Thomas didn't know what to say.

Finally Johannes broke the silence. "That'll be two wives I've buried."

"Oh, Father, this is tragic. What about the

girls? Do you want me to tell them?"

Johannes shrugged.

"Frances and Cicely are very upset about Eleanor's condition, and without Mrs. Woodbury here, I don't know how they'll react to losing her. I don't think I should go back to school and leave them," Thomas said.

"Then you should probably stay." After a moment of silence, Johannes added, "Do you think John will want to do the same?" His voice was soft and frail, unlike the bellows Thomas had heard throughout his childhood.

"I don't know, Father. I'll go find him and tell him what's happening."

"Very well. You do that." His voice trailed off.

As Thomas left the room, he glanced back to see his father still staring out the window with slumped shoulders. This was the very first time in Thomas's twenty-one years that his father looked mortal to him. Thomas had grown up in the presence of a roaring giant, an immortal man whose façade could not be splintered. The sight of a fragile old man staring out the window frightened and unnerved Thomas. He felt the world shift and realized it was time for him to step into the role of patriarch. He walked down the hall to find John.

John had his small trunk on top of his bed and was putting clothing into it.

"John, I've decided to stay here at Astwood until we know more about Eleanor's condition."

John stopped packing and turned to Thomas in the doorway. "Do you think she's really that bad?"

"The doctor said she is. He said to prepare

ourselves for the worst, and I think our sisters need a man here to support them."

John wrinkled his brow. "Father is here for them. I don't understand."

Thomas looked down at the floor. "I, um, well, I think our father is taking Eleanor's illness pretty hard."

"What do you mean? He doesn't take anything hard. He's only concerned with himself." John returned to his packing. He folded a silk shirt and tucked it into the trunk.

"John, he's not the tyrant you make him out to be, and besides, this situation is different. He looks weary and frightened." Thomas paused and squared his shoulders. "So, I think my presence is needed here. If you want to go ahead and return to London, do so, but I'm going to stay."

John stopped packing again. "Do you think I should stay, too?"

Thomas shrugged. "It's up to you."

Thomas turned to leave but John said, "What about Mary?"

"What about her?"

"Eleanor is her aunt. Do you think she is as distressed as our sisters?"

"I don't know but I would assume so. Perhaps you should find her and speak with her."

"Yes, I think I will."

John walked down the hall and heard his sisters and Mary talking in Cicely's sitting room. He entered the door which was ajar but stopped to await their greeting. All three girls stopped their stitching, turned toward him, and smiled. Cicely placed her needlework on the table and rose. "How is our stepmother doing today?"

John didn't respond for a moment, not knowing how much they knew, and certainly not wanting to alarm them. Frances's forehead furrowed as she sat, a piece of cloth in one hand, a floating needle in the other. Mary's face was pale and her eyes were red. He shook his head.

Mary's eyes closed and her shoulders shuddered. Cicely walked across the room and stood behind Mary's chair. She placed her hands on Mary's shoulders.

"I came here to tell you all something."

The girls stared at him. John looked from one to the other. Mary's tear-filled eyes twisted a place in John's heart he had never felt before.

"What is it?" Cicely asked.

He tore his attention away from Mary and cleared his throat. "Thomas and I have decided to stay at Astwood until we know more about Eleanor's condition. We will not be returning to Middle Temple right now."

"Oh, that's good news, John. I'm sure Father appreciates it," said Cicely.

Frances nodded in agreement.

John stood awkwardly in the doorway, not knowing what else to stay. It would be inappropriate for him to sit in the sewing circle with the ladies, but he was reluctant to leave Mary's side. He watched her dab her eyes with a handkerchief and resisted the urge to go to her. He wanted to talk with her. He wanted to hold her. He wanted to kiss away her tears. He wanted to touch her face and look into her eyes. He didn't understand what he was feeling for this girl. Her slight frame brought out the chivalry in him, the valor, and he wanted nothing more than to rescue this damsel from the cruelty of the truth.

Cicely's voice made him pull his eyes away from Mary. "Is there anything else, John?"

"Um, no, that's all," he stammered. He hadn't realized he had been staring at Mary, and now his sisters were eyeing him strangely. "I guess I'll be going, then."

He turned to leave the room.

"John?" Mary called softly.

His heart jumped. He turned back to look at her, knowing his face was flush with anticipation and embarrassment. His palms began to sweat.

"Would you take me to see my aunt?"

"Yes, Mary, I would be honored to escort you."

He held out his hand and waited for her to set her sewing down and walk toward him. When her cool fingers met his hot palm, he felt a tightening in his stomach. He escorted her down the hall to his stepmother's room.

She stopped outside the door, released his hand, and turned to him. "John, I know this will sound a little selfish and it's not how I mean for it to sound, but I don't have any other family. What shall happen to me if my aunt dies?"

He looked deep into her brown eyes and felt himself drowning in them. He would do whatever it took to protect this beautiful woman. "Don't worry, Mary, you have a place here. You will always have a place here. I'll see to it."

"Are you sure?"

He nodded and gave her a reassuring smile. "I'm sure."

He opened Eleanor's chamber door and led Mary to the bedside. She sat down on the chair next to the bed. John stood behind her chair and watched her take Eleanor's hand, which she stroked gently as her shoulders trembled with sobs. John knew at that moment he wanted to be by this girl's side for the rest of his life. He would demand that his father look after her until he graduated from Middle Temple. John would then look after her himself.

The next three weeks found John coming up with any excuse to be by Mary's side. They strolled in the winter garden, ate late suppers alone in the kitchen, sat by the fire while he read to her stories of swashbuckling sailors and pirates. He appeared at her door each morning to escort her to her aunt's sickbed. He refused to leave her side even when she sat for hours at her aunt's bedside. He wanted nothing more than to look into her brown eyes and smell the vanilla scent of her hair when she was close to him. Each evening, he escorted her to her chambers so she could retire for the night. He stood outside her door and listened to her sobs, wishing he could do more to comfort her.

On a damp and blustery February morning, the Culpepper family gathered under the timber bell-turret of St. John the Baptist Church in Mamble, Worcestershire, and buried Eleanor Culpepper among other members of the Blount family, next to her first husband, Sir George Blount.

Johannes Culpepper, Esquire, was once again a widower.

CHAPTER 16
1624, Middle Temple

"Why are you so quiet?" Thomas asked as the carriage rolled onto the grounds of Middle Temple.

"I'm wondering if we're still needed at home," John replied. The carriage came to a halt. He looked out the window but didn't move to exit.

"They'll be all right. Father will make sure of it."

"I know Cicely and Frances will be fine, but…" John rose and stepped out of the carriage. The late afternoon had grown so foggy that it was difficult to see the other end of the garden. John glanced at the spot across the lawn where a statue of one of Middle Temple's founding fathers surely stood, but he couldn't see it through the fog. The driver hopped down from the front and walked toward him. The driver asked if he should take the trunks to the boy's rooms. John nodded.

"But what?" Thomas emerged from the carriage, looking more like an elegant gentleman than a student in his velvet cloak and embroidered gloves.

"Oh, it's nothing." John sulked through the archway into Temple Garden with Thomas following close behind. The dingy stone walls, decorated at the base with winter's dead flowers, seemed to match John's somber mood.

"What is it, brother? Something is troubling you." Thomas quickened his pace to catch up.

John kept his head down, staring at the brown grass as he marched toward the library.

"John?"

John stopped and spun around and Thomas almost ran into him. "I was thinking about Mary."

"What about her? Father will take good care of her. She has no place else to go."

John looked as if he wanted to say something else, but he turned and resumed his trek toward the library.

"Wait, wait, wait." Thomas grabbed John's arm and stopped him. "You like that girl!" Thomas smiled.

"So what if I do?" John pulled away and continued walking.

Thomas quietly followed his little brother across the garden lawn. By the time they had rounded the library and reached their building, Thomas had replayed the entire visit home in his head and had come to terms with the fact his little brother was infatuated with a brown-eyed orphan. He couldn't believe he hadn't noticed. When they reached their residence door, Thomas said, "She's very pretty. I can see why you like her."

John didn't reply until they reached the second floor. He stopped in front of his chamber door and turned to Thomas. "I don't *like* her, Thomas. I am in love with her, deeply, head-over-heels, nothing-else-matters in love with her. I don't want to be here. I want to be with her."

Thomas's jaw dropped as he watched his little brother disappear into his room and slam the door

* * *

For the next year, when Thomas wasn't spending time at Leeds Castle with the beautiful Katherine St. Leger, he worked for his cousin, Sir Thomas Culpepper. He quickly learned the intricate tools of his trade and expanded his social circle to include other members of the bench. He was frequently invited to sup with his newfound colleagues, and one warm June evening, the subject at the table turned to the dissolution of the Virginia Company.

It had been founded in 1606 with the purpose of populating the colonies and amassing goods from the abundant natural resources found there. The aristocracy had been funding the ships for eighteen years and had yet to see a profit.

To entice sailors and settlers to travel to the new land, the Crown offered headrights. A headright was worth between one and one hundred acres of land in the new colony, depending on whether the traveler was a sailor or a settler. Many sailors worked numerous voyages in expectation of collecting enough headrights to trade for a sizeable plot of land, and many ship captains transported settlers across the ocean in exchange for their headrights, which could be sold or traded for goods.

Some settlers sailed at the expense of colony landowners, becoming indentured to the landowner for a specific amount of time to pay back the debt of passage. The landowner freely used the indentured person's headrights for the extent of the contract. When the contract ended, the indentured person would receive his rightful headrights and be set free from the contract, but not all landowners were honest, and there were countless instances of contracts being extended against the indentured person's will. No laws were in place to prevent this practice and the indentured person was ultimately at the mercy of the landowner.

The Virginia Company had been created to assist all involved—investors, sailors, settlers, and merchants, but after nearly two decades of not seeing a profit, the aristocracy refused to put any more money into it. Merchants and sailors became frustrated by the lack of pay they were promised, as there were no goods trading hands. Mortality rates of sailors and settlers climbed. King James, who would rather enjoy the pleasures of the hunt than worry about some distant colonies, grew tired of listening to the grievances of the aristocracy, the merchants, and the settlers, so with very little hesitation he disbanded the entire company.

Instead of the Virginia Colony being owned by and overseen by its investors, the king issued a new ruling declaring the Virginia Colony an English Crown Colony, owned solely by the Crown. He declared it to be self-governing by the people who lived there, and offered improved headrights—fifty acres for a new colonist and one hundred acres for a returning colonist—to anyone who would sail to the new land and settle it at their own expense.

"What does this mean for the shareholders?"

Thomas asked the men at the table.

"It means the certificate you have saying you're a shareholder isn't worth the paper it's written on," replied Sir Culpepper.

"Well, there's got to be something we can do about this legally," said Thomas.

"Not unless you want to battle the crown, which I wouldn't advise," one of the elder lawyers warned.

Most of the men around the table were original shareholders of the now defunct company, and the din grew louder as the men voiced their complaints and frustration. Thomas listened to them as he chugged his mug of ale, wondering what his father would say about this new proclamation. He knew Johannes had lost a small fortune financing the company, and he wondered if his father would be as distressed as the men surrounding him or happy it was over.

CHAPTER 17
March 27, 1625,
London

It began as any other day—a cool morning with bright sunshine and blue skies, complete with birds chirping from the trees. Then it began. It started with one church bell, then a second, then a third. After a few minutes, every church bell in the city pealed, and there was only one phrase on everyone's lips: The king is dead.

King James had suffered for years from arthritis, gout, and kidney stones. Everyone knew he was overly fond of his wine and had fainting fits, occasionally hitting his head when he collapsed. He had seldom visited London over the past year, and the rumor in Thomas's circle of parliamentary friends was that the king had recently suffered a stroke and had become severely disabled.

At the beginning of King James's rule, he had assured the people that he would not persecute anyone if they remained silent about their religious practices and obeyed the law that required citizens to take an oath of allegiance to the king, denying the pope's authority over the king. He initially demanded the abolition of confirmation and the term "priest," but his strict enforcement had eased as his reign continued. His eldest son, Prince Charles, would now be declared King Charles I of England, Scotland, and Ireland, and after twenty-two years of King James's peaceful and scholarly rule, everyone cautiously hoped Charles Stuart would follow in his father's footsteps.

John and Mary had exchanged many letters since her aunt passed away, but the death of the king gave John a new excuse to write her. He sent a letter immediately.

My dearest Mary,

I'm sure you have heard by now that King James has died at his home at Theobalds Palace, and everyone here in London is greatly distraught. I remember visiting the palace a few years ago when my cousin JC was knighted. It is a magnificent estate and I hope to see it again someday.

I trust that you are well and my sisters are taking very good care of you. I miss your aunt Eleanor with every passing day, as I am sure you do also.

Please write with the news from home when you can.

Yours truly,

John Culpepper

A few weeks later, John received a letter from Astwood Court.

My dearest John,

Yes, we heard about the king and are deeply saddened. We also heard King Charles's coronation will be held next year, following the Yuletide celebration. I would certainly love to see something so grand. How often does one witness such a spectacle?

I'm not sure if Cicely or Frances has written you about the events at Astwood Court, so what I am about to share may come as a great surprise to you. Your father has remarried. The woman's name is Ann Goddard. She is nearly half your father's age, but she seems to make him happy. He has a smile on his face again, which I haven't seen since my dear aunt passed away. Ann is a widow and has a teenage son who is away at school, and she seems to be a very well-appointed woman with a good background. Would you think your father would marry any less?

I hope you can return to Astwood for the summer. I worry so about you and Thomas when I hear rumors of the plague growing in the city. Your father said the Council has sent in searchers to each parish to determine the cause of death for anyone who has died within the last month. He says they fear the plague will be very bad this summer.

I wish you well and hope to see you soon.
Yours,
Mary

As feared in Mary's letter, by June the plague had spread throughout all of London and into the nearby towns. John packed his belongings to return to Astwood Court for the remainder of the summer. Thomas refused to accompany him, as he had decided to spend the summer at Leeds Castle with Katherine St. Leger and Uncle Alexander.

When John arrived at Astwood, his new stepmother greeted him at the door. She was indeed half their father's age but seemed kind enough, with hair the color of sand and a soft, watery complexion. She had neither rose in her cheeks nor sparkle in her eye, and was more homely than John thought appropriate for his father's taste. After all, Ursula and Eleanor had been stunningly beautiful women who always had an air of vivacity about them.

"Good afternoon, Mistress Ann, or would you like me to call you stepmother?" John took her hands in his own.

She smiled. "Ann is fine. I doubt you need another mother at your age."

He kissed her on both cheeks. "Very well, then. It is my pleasure to make your acquaintance, Ann."

"And mine. Can I make you some warm cider?"

"Um, no, but thank you for the offer. I need to see my, um, father right away," he fibbed. He dropped his cloak and hat on the chair in the doorway and bolted up the stairs. While it was pleasant meeting his new stepmother, there was only one person in the house he was truly anxious to see.

He tiptoed down the hallway and heard the lilt of the girls' voices coming from Cicely's room. He rapped on her door.

"Come in," called Cicely.

John flung open the door and scanned the large room for the object of his affection. Cicely and Frances jumped up and ran to greet their brother, but Mary rose shyly and remained standing next to her tapestry-covered chair. A blush rose in her cheeks, matching the shade of her pink gown. Her dark hair framed her beautiful face as she lowered her head to avoid John's gaze.

After he hugged his sisters, he ignored their chatter and questions and headed straight toward Mary. He wrapped his arms around her. Her blush darkened to a deep crimson, but she hugged him back. He softly placed a kiss on both cheeks and smiled radiantly at her. When one of his sisters cleared her throat, he turned and saw Cicely and Frances staring at him in disbelief.

"John," said Cicely. "We didn't know you were so fond of Mary."

Now it was John's turn to blush. "Well, I've missed all of you."

Frances giggled as she returned to her seat, picked up her sewing, and sat down. Cicely crossed the room and wrapped her arms around her brother's elbow. She walked toward the door, pulling him away from Mary.

"Well, with your boldness, I hope she is just as fond of you." She glanced over her shoulder and gave Mary a wink. "Have you met our new stepmother?"

John allowed Cicely to lead him toward the door, but he glanced back and was happy to see Mary watching him. He smiled and nodded at her, indicating he would see her later when Cicely was done with whatever she was up to. "Yes, sister, Ann greeted me when I arrived."

"Good. I was going to write to you and tell you all about her, but Mary said she had already done so. Let's go downstairs. I'd like to see Thomas."

He stopped walking. "Thomas didn't come with me."

"He didn't? Why not?" She pouted.

"He decided to spend the summer at Uncle Alexander's."

"Oh, I would love to see our dear uncle. How is he?" Cicely pulled John close to her and resumed walking.

"I'm sure he's just fine, and he'd probably love to see you also."

When they reached the top of the stairs, John glanced back again. Mary was standing in the doorway, watching them walk down the hall. She looked like an angel and his heart fluttered. He couldn't wait for the opportunity to be alone with her.

CHAPTER 18
January 1626,
Middle Temple

Due to the plague, John remained at Astwood Court all through the fall and didn't return to Middle Temple until late January. Sickness and death had ravaged London for months and taken thousands of lives. Anyone who had the means to leave the city did so, and school had closed until the end of Yuletide. When John returned for his final semester, he found a letter waiting for him on his desk. It was from his brother. Thomas wrote that he had been offered a position as a bencher and would not be returning to school. Thomas had spent the summer at Leeds Castle, and thanks to Uncle Alexander's connections, had been offered positions with a few different barristers and was soon expected to be called to the bar himself.

John tossed the letter on his desk and collapsed on his bed. He sighed deeply and stared at the ceiling. How would he survive Middle Temple without his brother's company? Why did everything seem to go as planned for Thomas? In contrast to his brother's numerous successes, John had been offered only a few minor positions as a clerk, and he had turned every one of them down. He did not want to be a lawyer. Everyone knew that. He was only attending Middle Temple to please his father which was a losing proposition.

After feeling sorry for himself for a few minutes, he rose and went next door to find Will Berkeley. He knocked on Will's door but Will didn't answer. He tried the handle and found the door unlocked. He poked his head in and saw the room was bare. Did Will get expelled?

He walked down the hall to Jasper's room but found it empty as well. He galloped down the steps and out the door. He went next door to the library and approached a table of students.

"Have you any word on Will Berkeley? His room is empty."

"Will was offered a position with a barrister. He said he won't be returning to school," a freckle-faced boy answered.

"That's too bad. My brother isn't coming back, either. I guess it's just me and Jasper, then."

"Oh, you haven't heard," the student said.

"Heard what?" John asked.

There was a long silence as knowing glances were exchanged around the table.

"What happened?" John asked.

"John, I'm very sorry to have to tell you this, but Jasper Churchyard and his father both died of the plague."

John felt as if someone had punched him in the stomach. "Jasper is dead?"

"Yes, I'm afraid so," the freckled boy said.

John walked away without another word.

Jasper died of the plague? Why didn't I take him with me? I should have demanded he come to Astwood Court. Why didn't I offer? What was I thinking? He marched across the garden and stopped at the place where he had picketed the goat. He looked down at the dead grass. A suffocating wave of guilt washed over him. It was because of him that Jasper stayed in London. It was because of him Jasper was dead. It was his fault. He had been too concerned with himself, too wrapped up in his desire to see Mary to even consider anyone else's safety. Tears welled up in his eyes and a hole formed in the pit of his stomach. He clomped across the lawn, heading toward Temple Church. He had never been a devoutly religious person but he didn't know what else to do.

He pushed open the heavy wooden door and entered the five-hundred-year-old church. He had never been inside, so he wasn't sure where to go. He looked up at the ornate rounded ceilings of the nave as he walked forward. When he reached the front of the church, he had to step around marble effigies of knights that rested on the floor. He admired their beauty and wondered how long they had been there.

Behind the effigies sat an altar filled with candles. He knelt on the bench in front of them and lit one for Jasper. He closed his eyes and whispered, "I'm so sorry, Jasper. I let you down. I should have taken better care of you. I'm heartbroken to lose you. You were a good boy and you would have grown to be a good man, but your life was cut too short." He looked down and saw dark spots from tears on his coat. "You will be missed, my dear friend."

Later that day, John sat in Headmaster

Barnaby's class with no cohorts by his side. Thinking about Barnaby as a goat had lost its appeal as there was no one to laugh with, no one to play pranks with. It seemed to John that he was the only student in the history of Middle Temple who was not benefiting from his education.

The only bright spots in his otherwise dismal existence were letters from Mary. She regaled him with stories of his sisters, his new stepmother, and his father, who had been named Sheriff of Worcestershire and was serving as presiding magistrate at quarter sessions. John wouldn't have even known about this if it wasn't for Mary, as the man had never sent John one letter.

Mary was quite an exquisite writer. The excitement in her words captured John's heart. Every depiction, every portrayal, every nuance was brilliant and charming. John wished he could receive a letter from her every day, but receiving a letter meant writing one in reply. John had nothing exciting to write back. He attended classes, ate alone in the corner of the hall, and spent most of his time in solitude as a majority of the boys of his class had obtained professional positions.

Daily, he walked down to the Thames to admire the ships. He spoke with deck hands about their impending voyages, questioning their supplies, routes, and navigational techniques. He remained on the waterfront until either the ships had set sail or the evening grew late. He dreaded walking back to school and never left the dockyard until he absolutely had to. The sounds of the creaking hulls rubbing against the taut ropes, the water lapping against the bows, and the smells of the raw materials being loaded into the ships drove him mad with passion. The tar, the fish, the cackle of the seabirds made him giddy. He wished he could express his excitement in writing as elegantly as Mary did.

He sat down at his small desk and wrote to Mary, regaling his latest experience at the docks. He told her how he had spent the day discussing inventory with a sailor and how he had been invited aboard one of the wooden beauties. Without too much bravado in his written words, he describe how exciting it was to be aboard a ship and how he longed for the crew to untie the ropes and set the sails. Though he was happy to be writing to her, he would give anything to finally be sailing instead of back in his dank room penning a letter by dim candlelight.

Mary's responding letter contained many questions about the ships. She inquired about the kind of supplies they were taking and how long they would be at sea. She asked how they navigated and what the sails were made of. She seemed genuinely interested in the business of ships, and John was happily surprised and eager to answer her questions. She was the very first person in his life who seemed as fascinated as he by the thought of sailing the seas.

Their letters became more and more frequent, not only containing countless tales of sailors, ships, and supplies, but also becoming more intimate. His feelings for her had grown immensely over the last two years, and he longed to see her again. He could tell from her letters the feelings were mutual.

By the end of the year, John had finished school and was packing for the final time to return to Astwood Court. As he was closing his trunk, JC appeared in his doorway.

"JC! What are you doing here?"

"John! I'm glad I found you. I came to ask you to accompany me somewhere."

"Where?"

"The king's coronation."

John's mouth opened and closed, but no words came. He had never attended anything as grand as a king's coronation.

JC grinned. "I'll tell you what we'll do, young cousin. We will forego Yuletide at Astwood Court this year and spend it here in London. We'll drink and dine in the taverns and dance with the fair maidens at court, and then we'll go to Westminster Abbey and attend the coronation. You will be amazed at the grandeur of the event, and it's something you only get to see once in your lifetime. Following the ceremony, you can meet King Charles's new wife, Henrietta Maria. She's caused quite a stir at court, if you don't know. She's from France and is…" He paused and leaned closer to John. "Well, she's Catholic. Parliament is beside itself that he didn't take the Spanish bride he had promised."

"What difference does it make?"

"What difference?" JC gawked at John. "The people of this country would rather die than go back under the pope's authority, and word is that Henrietta Maria will push her Catholic agenda on the king and the court. The whole mess could take us back to the Tudor era, where one could be beheaded just for thinking in a different religion than the monarchy. It makes quite a big difference."

"Oh, I didn't realize it was that bad."

"It's that bad all right. The king has refused to convene Parliament before his coronation because he doesn't want any trouble from them. There's quite a power struggle going on at court right now." JC looked down the hall for eavesdroppers and lowered his voice. "My advice to you, young cousin, is to get on the king's good side from the beginning. It's the only true protection for any of us. My plan is to become Privy Counselor as soon as possible, and maybe Master of the Rolls someday soon. Not to turn the king's ear but to keep mine to the ground for disquiet in the land."

John's forehead wrinkled. "Disquiet?"

JC nodded. "You never know when a civil war will break out, especially when the people in power are divided like they are now. So, I'm looking to increase my position at court, for my own safety if nothing else."

"You'll do it, JC. You always achieve whatever you aspire to."

JC smiled. "So, it's settled, then. Yuletide in London, followed by the king's coronation at Westminster Abbey."

"Sure, that'll be great."

John took his things to JC's apartment and wrote a letter to Mary about his plans. A few weeks later, he received a response.

> *Dearest John,*
> *I am saddened that you won't be coming home for Yuletide, but I am pleased that you will spend it with*

JC, especially at Westminster. I'm sure the coronation will be exciting and no doubt impressive. Please write and tell me every detail of it and the Yuletide festivities you attend. I know this will sound silly, but please describe Princess Henrietta Maria's gown. Your sisters and I are dying to know what she wears and how grand she looks.
With much love and affection,
Mary

With Mary's blessing and JC by his side, John spent weeks eating and drinking like royalty and traveling from pub to pub, trying to keep up with his cousin, who was skilled at living the high life. John was more than a little exhausted by the time coronation day arrived. He and JC traveled to Westminster and took their seats in the back of the abbey, readying themselves for the grandest event they would ever witness in their lifetimes.

CHAPTER 19
February 2, 1626

John sat next to JC, watching the proceedings in awe. People around them whispered that Henrietta Maria would not be in attendance today, for she had adamantly refused to attend the Protestant ceremony. The spectators didn't come right out and scoff at her Catholic beliefs or lack of participation in the ceremony, for that could be dangerously construed as treason, but it was mentioned that at the very least she could have made an appearance to show support for her husband. John got the distinct feeling the new queen was not well liked in London, and he was certain his sisters and Mary would be disappointed when he sent word that the queen hadn't attended.

When the trumpets blared from the doorway, JC tapped John on the leg and whispered, "Here they come!"

The procession began with choir boys singing as they walked up the aisle and took their place at the front of the chapel. John wasn't counting, but there had to be one hundred of them. Next to enter was a group of men walking two by two, dressed in colorful robes denoting their various positions. JC whispered some of their names, positions, and titles to John as they passed. First were the aldermen, then eighty Knights of the Bath, followed by the king's serjeants-at-law, the solicitor, and attorney general. Following them were judges, barons, bishops, and viscounts. Then came the members of Parliament. A few smiled. Most looked a bit disgruntled. John recognized many of their faces but knew only a few of their names. He was certain JC knew every name and imagined Thomas would know them also. Following the members of Parliament were the officers of the state, including eight earls and one marquis. One carried a sword, one the globe, one the scepter, and one the king's crown. The lord mayor of London entered next, carrying the short scepter, and then two bishops joined the procession, carrying the golden cup and plate for communion. John thought his legs would give out before all the important people had entered. He just wanted to see the new king. The earl of Arundel and the duke of Buckingham passed next. John looked around at the crowd and noticed some of the faces growing pale. He was glad he wasn't the only one growing fatigued by the length of the procession.

Finally, the music changed and John glanced at JC, who looked as if he would jump out of his skin in excitement. They smiled at each other and turned back toward the door. The king entered, and John had never seen anyone look as stately.

The king's dark hair flowed onto his shoulders, covering the white satin collar on his violet cape. Under the cape, the king's entire wardrobe was white, and he glowed like an angel as he stood in the sunshine cascading through the doorway. He was presented with the staff of King Edward. He took it and waited for his escorts to take their places. A colorful canopy rose above his head, its four corners held by the four barons of the ports. Bishops took their places, flanking the king. The train of his purple velvet cape was lifted on either corner by the master of the robes and the master of the wardrobe. When his entourage was in place, he slowly marched toward the front of the church. The choir continued singing as the archbishop of Canterbury presented His Majesty to the Lords and Commons. After they gave their consent to his coronation and he had taken his seat, the sermon began.

John thought he would doze off as the bishop droned on and on. Perhaps it would have been more interesting if he could hear what the man was saying, but all John could hear from the back of the long church was a low mumble of Latin that occasionally included the word Christus. He wondered how he could word the description in his letter to Mary to make the coronation sound more exciting than it was.

Finally, after a prayer and another song from the choir, the sermon was finished and the king stepped to the altar to take his oath. In the back of the church, this part of the ceremony wasn't any clearer than the sermon had been, but when it was over, the horns blared again from the doorway and the church bells rang the announcement to all of London. The crowd rose to its feet as the king followed the procession back to the front door. This time, he wore a magnificent crown covered with glittering jewels. Each head bowed as the king passed.

Following the crowd that was like a herd of cattle squeezing through a single gate, John and JC eventually emerged from the church. By the time they reached the street, the king was already astride his white horse and trotting through the multitude of people lining either side of the road. When the king waved, the crowd cheered even louder than the ringing church bells.

John couldn't wait to get back to JC's apartment and write to Mary.

CHAPTER 20
Fall 1626,
Astwood Court

John entered his sister's bedroom and reached for her hands. "Frances, my dearest little sister, you have transformed into a beautiful bride. You are absolutely glowing." He kissed her cheeks.

"I have transformed because I am in love, brother. I'm sorry you haven't been home to become acquainted with my betrothed."

"I'm sure if you love him, he's perfect. And Father approves?"

Frances beamed as Cicely fluffed out the hem of her dress. "Yes, Father adores him."

"Well, tell me—what makes him so special?"

"Special to me or to Father?" She rolled her eyes.

"Both."

"Well, for Father, James Medlicote comes from a very affluent family. He is a lawyer and will undoubtedly support me in the lifestyle to which I am accustomed." She raised her chin as if she were royalty.

John laughed. His little sister was always on

stage.

Frances continued. "And of course Father is excited to have another lawyer in the family."

John looked down at their entwined fingers and cleared his throat. "Um, yes, I'm sure he is."

Frances froze. "Oh, John, I'm sorry. I didn't mean anything."

He smiled. "I know you didn't. Now continue. What is it you love about this Mr. Medlicote?"

She released his hands and twirled around the room like a young girl on a dance floor. "He is dashing. He has warm, brown eyes and teeth as white as pearls. His smile melts my heart. And he's very good to me, as kind as any man could be. He's gentle and sweet and…"

John roared with laughter. "That's enough, my dear sister. It's obvious you are madly in love with this young man. I wish you all the happiness the world can give you." He reached for her again.

Frances wrapped her arms around his neck and kissed him on the cheek. "Thank you, John. Your blessing means everything to me."

The family boarded three carriages and traveled to St. John the Baptist Church to witness Frances's marriage to James Medlicote. The young couple grinned at each other through the entire service. Johannes sat next to Ann in the second pew and beamed with pride. John looked down the row at him, wondering if he could ever do anything that would elicit a response like that from the man. Johannes looked back at John and frowned. There was John's answer.

After the ceremony, Frances and James exited

the church, followed closely by Cicely carrying her little sister's train. Johannes and Ann came out next, and then Thomas and Katherine, and John and Mary. The family boarded the carriages, bound for a celebration at Ragley Castle. Since there were only three carriages, the newlywed couple took one, Johannes, his wife, and the girls took the second, and John rode with Thomas and Katherine.

Ragley Castle was the home of a family friend, and Johannes had arranged for Frances's reception to be held in the main hall.

"Oh my goodness! Look at this place," said Katherine when they arrived. "It's bigger than Leeds Castle."

"I think you're right. It's enormous," said Thomas.

John didn't comment as he looked at the magnificent mansion before them. It had no fewer than thirty windows across its facade and four fifty-foot Romanesque columns gracing the entrance. The place was breathtaking indeed, complete with peacocks strutting around the front lawn. Johannes had outdone himself.

A gourmet meal was lavished upon the nearly two hundred guests, wine flowed like water, and an orchestra played until late into the evening. Women in exquisitely embroidered gowns were escorted around the dance floor by men in well-appointed doublets and breeches. Family and friends had come from miles around to attend the festivities, and Johannes had spared no expense providing the best of everything for his youngest daughter.

John watched his father greet the guests. The man strutted around the room like a king, conversing with barons and earls and the local gentry. Something about Johannes's demeanor seemed arrogant and haughty, making John wonder if the opulence of the celebration was to honor his sister's marriage or if it was to show the neighbors how prosperous the Culpepper family was.

As the sun began to set and the partygoers bid their good-byes, Cicely hugged John and told him she would see him at home in the morning.

"Is Father driving you home?"

"Yes, Mary and I are riding in his carriage."

"If you wouldn't mind, I'd like to ask Mary to ride with me."

Cicely smiled. "She likes you, you know. She lights up like the sun every time she receives word from you."

"I feel the same way." He was thankful for the dim light in the hall to hide the blush that had covered his face.

"You should mention it to Father. He has no idea what is going on between you two. It's obvious you're not going to follow the family tradition and become a lawyer, and Father's prepared to lose you to the sea. I'm sure he'd rather lose you to Mary."

"I don't want to be a lawyer."

"I know, and so does everyone else, but I don't think it would be fair for Mary to love a husband who lives at sea."

"Husband?"

"That's what people do, John. They fall in love and get married."

John stared at her. He had never considered marriage, and certainly hadn't considered how he would support a wife—with or without going to sea.

Cicely rose on her tiptoes and kissed her brother on the cheek. "It'll work out, John. It always does." She turned toward the door, and then turned back. "But you still should tell Father."

"Tell him what?" Mary asked as she approached John to say good-bye.

John smiled at her. "Um, tell him I was going to offer to take you home. I have my carriage here."

"Oh, I would love that, John."

John and Mary, arm in arm, went to find Johannes. They found him in the ballroom.

"Father, I will be escorting Mary home if that's all right with you."

"Very well. I'll see you there." Johannes kissed Mary on the cheek but barely acknowledged John. John wasn't surprised. Johannes had been ignoring him all day, except for the occasional angry look.

"Good night." Mary said as she wrapped her arm around John's elbow.

"Good night, my dear," Johannes replied and turned to speak with guests.

John escorted Mary to his carriage. He told the driver to take the long way around the town. He helped Mary into the carriage, and the two remained silent as they listened to the horses clopping on the dry road.

"May I ask you a question, John?" Mary asked softly.

"Of course."

"What is happening between you and your father?"

"Oh, he's just upset that I don't want to sit on the bench. I think he's angry he can't control me."

"Why don't you want to practice law?"

John sighed. "That's a long story that has nothing to do with law, but more to do with my father and my upbringing. He was a lawyer and was never home when I was a child. I guess I resent that. I don't want to be the same kind of man."

"But you want to sail a ship?"

"Yes." This was a topic of discussion John liked immensely more than talking about his father.

"Do you think you'd be home with your children any more than your father was?"

"Well, truthfully, I've never really given it much thought. I just know in my heart I don't want to be a lawyer. I don't want to be like my father."

John waited for her to ask him more about ships, but she didn't. John changed the subject and for the next hour made small talk about his sister's wedding, the guests, and Ragley Castle, but Mary gave him only one-word answers.

"You're being unusually quiet, Mary. Is everything all right?"

"Oh, I'm sorry. I think I need to be more cautious."

"Cautious?"

"Yes."

"Why would you need to be cautious around me? You know I have the best of intentions."

"Yes, I know you do, but with all of our letters to and from each other, I've come to realize...well, how do I say this?" She paused. "I've come to realize that nothing will ever be as great in your life as your love of ships, and no woman will ever be as important to you as the sea."

"The sea? Important?" After her words sunk in, he reached for her hand and said, "Yes, my dream of sailing is important to me, but the sea can't give me children, she can't keep me warm at night, and she will never love me in return."

Mary stared out the window. She was so beautiful in the glow of the setting sun, and he hoped he wasn't saying the wrong things. The tension in his chest grew as large as the silence between them. He had just declared his love for her—well, in a roundabout sort of way. Wasn't she going to say anything? Was she going to leave him sitting here with his heart in his hands?

Finally, she cleared her throat. "I can certainly give you all those things, John, but I would hate to be left alone to raise children while my husband was off sailing the world with his mistress."

John smiled. "You could come with me."

"On a ship?" She huffed. "Women don't do such things, John. People die on ships all the time. Disease and sickness take almost as many sailors as the ones who arrive safely at their destination."

"Women can sail, and with everything I've learned, I know how to command a vessel safely. There will be no sickness or disease or dying on any ship under my command."

"You sound so confident, like you've been sailing for years and years. That's why I know you'll be a great captain." She paused. "But I don't want to live on a ship. I don't want to raise children on a ship. And I don't want to live alone while my husband sails away for months or years at a time. How could I survive each day not knowing if you would ever come home again?"

He looked down at their entwined fingers. "I don't think you need to worry about it."

"Why not?"

"I approached my father this morning and asked for financing to buy a ship, and he in no ambiguous terms told me no. He was so angry, he even threatened to disown me."

"Oh, no. That's why you two were glaring at each other all day. You should have told me."

"There's nothing you can do, Mary. Johannes Culpepper is a stubborn man with a fierce temper. One can't negotiate with him. Thomas is the heir to my father's estates, and I will get nothing. I don't have the funds to purchase a ship, and I know I'll never be able to get through to him to help me." John's voice cracked.

"But you still have your law studies."

"That's useless. Law school was a waste of four years of my life."

"Certainly it has not been a waste. I'm sure you could secure a position with a barrister if you choose. If not, you can certainly work for Thomas when he gets his own practice."

John looked out the window. Perhaps she was right. Perhaps the only place for the second son was to work for the first son. His future held very limited possibilities. There would be no title, no inheritance, no money, no lands, and no possibility of achieving any childhood dream, especially one as large as a ship.

No, she couldn't be right. This couldn't be all there was to life. What about seeing the world? What about adventure? His dreams couldn't be rubbish, as his father had bellowed that morning. But if he could somehow find a way to buy a ship, what would it all mean if he had to live without the woman he loved? Perhaps both Mary and his father were right. The thought made him sick. Perhaps everyone had been right his whole life. Maybe the sea was no place for a Culpepper. Maybe he should put more effort into securing a position on the bench, if for nothing else than the love of the beautiful woman sitting next to him.

He looked at her and saw her head bob with each dip in the road. In his silence, she had dozed off. He rubbed his thumb across her gloved knuckles and listened to the soft sound of her rhythmic breathing. He knew one thing for certain. If he had to give up his dream of captaining a ship, she would be the reason, and she would be worth it.

CHAPTER 21
1627, Astwood Court

Thomas ran into the library, out of breath and face flushed.

John was sitting in front of the fireplace reading a book. He looked up at his brother. "My goodness! What is it, Thomas? You look like you're running from a wild boar." John closed the book and placed it on the table beside his chair.

"I don't know which news to tell you first." Thomas looked as if he would pop out of his skin.

"Tell me the most boring news first and save the best for last."

"Um, all right. The boring news is that I've been offered my own chambers at Middle Temple. I am now officially Thomas Culpepper, Esquire."

John jumped up and shook his brother's hand. "What?! That is fabulous news, brother. Everything you've worked so hard for has finally come to fruition. Congratulations!"

"I can't believe it myself." Thomas smiled and shook his head.

"Wait, so that's not the good news?"

"No, actually there are two more things."

"Two? Well, tell me before you explode."

"Father told me when I became a lawyer he would give me Greenway Court."

"Our childhood home?" John knew the day would come when Thomas would begin taking over Culpepper estates, but the news caused a mixture of emotions. He was certainly happy for his brother's success, but felt a deep melancholy that the property he had loved so much as a child now belonged to someone else.

"Yes, Greenway Court is mine now."

"That's wonderful news, but you already knew that was coming, right?"

Thomas shrugged. "Well, yes, but…" Thomas grinned like John had never seen him grin before.

"But what? What are you smiling about?"

"I'm going to go live there very soon." Thomas's face turned as red as a turnip and John thought his brother was losing his mind.

"Of course you are. What is going on?"

"I'm moving there with my wife!"

"Your wife. What wife?"

"Katherine St. Leger. Uncle Alexander gave us his blessing."

John was speechless. His brother was now a practicing lawyer with his own business and the lord of a major country estate, and he was in love with a woman he was apparently going to marry. Why was everything going for Thomas as effortlessly as if it were a scene in a play? Why did all the men in the Culpepper family dictate their futures so flawlessly, just as JC had done when they were children? Why couldn't John make this happen for himself?

* * *

A month later, as summer's kiss opened every flower and birds danced with joy, John and Mary walked arm in arm through the rose garden on the south side of Astwood Court. Butterflies danced on the fragrant aroma of red and white rosebuds, and the afternoon sun bathed them in warmth. Behind them, the three-story manor house stood as a lone beacon in a sea of green pastures.

"I've been thinking a lot lately about a conversation I had with Thomas and about what you said about being the wife of a sailor, and I've realized that such a life would surely not be fitting for you," John said without looking at her.

Mary waited for him to continue.

"I've made a decision that will affect both of us." He could tell she was holding her breath so he wanted to say what was on his mind as quickly as possible. "I've decided to devote my energy to my law career. Since Thomas received his own chambers at Middle Temple, I was thinking it would be appropriate for me to ask him for a position."

"Really, John? That sounds so promising." She tried to hide the excitement in her voice, but John knew her well enough to know when she was holding back.

"It's not exactly what I dreamed of doing with my life, but it's the only way I can think of to ensure that you'll be by my side, and that's the most important thing to me."

"And there is nothing more important to me."

He stopped walking and pulled her to face him, holding on to her elbows. He gazed at her intensely, admiring the way the sun made her brown hair shine like silk.

"I'm going to establish myself in London." He paused. "And then we will be together."

She smiled and her eyes danced with joy. "I can't wait."

"I can't wait either. I promise you I will work tirelessly to secure my position. It won't be too long."

"John, I have already waited several years for you to finish school. I think I can wait a little while longer."

He tilted up her chin with his forefinger and edged toward her. He melted into her eyes, the soft fragrance of vanilla enveloping his senses like a cloud. He looked from her eyes to her lips and she didn't pull away or blush. He had waited for this moment for so long. He inched forward and softly kissed her lips. She opened her parasol in one fluid movement and placed it above their heads while they shared their first kiss in the middle of the sunny rose garden.

The following night, after the family had finished supper, Thomas raised his glass and proudly announced that he and Katherine St. Leger were to be married immediately at Leeds Castle. The family toasted the coming union, and the volume of their excitement increased as they discussed plans for the wedding.

John glanced at Mary across the table and saw her eyes darken at the fact she was not the bride being toasted. He grinned at her, a dimple creasing his cheek, and he mouthed, "Soon."

CHAPTER 22
July 10, 1628,
Thomas and Katherine

The family gathered in the south chapel of St. John the Baptist Church in Harrietsham where they sat quietly in the ragstone building on wooden pews and waited for the ceremony to begin. The bishop entered first, followed by Thomas and John. Thomas took his place near the altar. John thought his brother looked as if he may faint at any moment, so John stood close by. Thomas watched the door and his face lit up. John followed his gaze and saw Katherine enter the front door of the church. She looked like a princess in her gold-embroidered silk gown which enhanced the rich auburn of her hair and her green eyes.

Cicely and Frances followed close behind her, each carrying a corner of her train. When they reached the front of the church, the girls took their places on the opposite side of the nave, and Katherine stood next to Thomas. She blushed and looked down at the floor as Thomas stared at her. Admiring how much his brother loved this woman, John glanced around the room to find Mary. She was seated in the second pew next to Johannes and Ann. John caught her eye and smiled. In his eyes, she looked more radiant than the bride and he found it hard to keep his eyes off of her. Johannes gave him a foul look but John didn't react to it. His love for Mary had nothing to do with his father.

After the ceremony, the family descended on Leeds Castle, where Uncle Alexander threw the party of the year. Lords and ladies filled the banqueting room while members of Parliament discussed business in the reception rooms. John and Mary kept to themselves at a table in a quiet corner.

The next morning, a breakfast fit for the king himself was served in the main hall, followed by an evening that resembled the one before. The party lasted for three days.

Thomas and Katherine moved into Greenway Court, and in October they invited the entire family to visit. Johannes and Ann, Cicely, Frances and James, John and Mary, and Uncle Alexander gathered at the estate. At the conclusion of the first family supper in their new home, Thomas tapped on the rim of his glass to get everyone's attention.

"Katherine and I are so pleased that you all could join us in our new home. We trust you all had a pleasant journey getting here, and please know that you are welcome to stay for as long as you like. We invited everyone because we have some news." He gestured for Katherine to stand by his side. "We would like to inform you that Katherine is with child and we are expecting the first Culpepper grandchild." Thomas beamed like a ray of sunshine.

Johannes rose and patted him on the back. "Thomas, Katherine, we are overjoyed by this news, and let me be the first to wish you a healthy son." Johannes raised his glass and the gathering followed his lead.

From across the table, John watched the interaction between his brother and his father, and wondered if he would have received the same hearty congratulations if it were him announcing the arrival of the first grandchild. He glanced at Mary and found her staring at him. He smiled faintly, but knew by the way she cocked her head that she recognized something was amiss.

As the rest of the family moved into the reception room to drink and talk, John grabbed Mary's hand and asked her to go for a walk in the garden. Her skin glowed golden in the sunset. He knew if she caught his eye, she would ask him what he had been thinking during Thomas's speech, so he walked with his head down, staring at the gravel path and fallen leaves beneath their feet.

Since the moment John arrived at Greenway Court, he had been barraged with memories of his childhood. He had been only five years old when they moved to Astwood Court, but spending time in these rooms and seeing the tapestries and artwork brought back many recollections that John had thought were long forgotten. Most were pleasant remembrances of life with his mother and siblings. There were also memories of a robust Mrs. Woodbury scrubbing him behind the ears and tucking him into bed.

But there were also painful memories. Memories of sitting on the front stoop until dark, awaiting his father's arrival. The evenings had always settled into blackness when Mrs. Woodbury would come out to gather him and bring him inside for the night. He often cried himself to sleep on those lonely nights, wondering why his father never tucked him into bed, took him riding, or shared meals with him. He tried to remember times in the house that included his father but couldn't come up with any. Not one.

"Are you all right, John?" Mary asked softly as she looped her arms around the crook of his elbow.

"I'm fine. I just keep finding myself drawn into childhood memories in this house." He looked off into the sunset. The autumn sky was turning brilliant shades of gold and pink and purple.

"That's right, you grew up here for a time, didn't you?"

"Yes, until I was five. I don't remember most of it, just bits and pieces. It's kind of like fragments of a puzzle that I can't quite piece together. Almost like a dream."

Mary hugged John's arm tighter as she glanced sideways at his face, then followed his gaze toward the sunset. "Something bothers you about the remembrances, though. What is it?"

"Nothing I can put my finger on." He shook his head and looked down at the gravel again. "I guess I just can't figure out why my father isn't present in any of my memories."

"Your father works day and night now. I'm sure he did the same when you were small. Are you sure he was even here?"

John stopped and turned toward her. "I think that's it. He wasn't here, ever. He was always in London, always working."

Mary turned to walk again and John allowed himself to follow her. After a few moments of only the crunch of the leaves beneath their feet, she said, "I imagine it's hard to grow up without a father."

He nodded.

"I guess that's why I was so concerned with you wanting to own a ship. What if you were never there to see our children grow? Would they feel the same about you in their childhood memories?"

"But my father should have been home with his family. He wasn't off sailing a ship. He was working right here in town, yet he never came home." He looked off in the distance at the massive oaks, expecting to witness the last of their red and gold leaves, but all he saw was their black silhouette of bare branches against the red sky. How can colors as vibrant as red and gold become black as night? His memories seemed the same.

When they reached the end of the garden, they turned to walk back to the house. Mary remained silent to let him work through his thoughts.

Finally, he said, "You know, when I was young and mentioned to JC that I wanted to own a ship someday, he teased me and said I would outgrow that desire. I didn't know what he meant at the time, but all of the men in my family seem to accomplish great things. JC has become a great knight for the monarchy. Thomas has married and established a successful law practice." He paused. "And now, he's expecting his first child. What have I done with my life so far? Nothing but dream of owning a ship. I've always known my father wouldn't allow it to happen. Maybe I carried that dream all this time just to get my father's attention."

"That's an interesting thought. Maybe you did."

He shrugged. "I realized since being back in this house it's time for me to grow up, to let go of my childhood dream. I will never be the heir to my father's estates. I will never have the fortune to buy a ship. I am holding the one woman I love at arm's length while I wait for my life to begin." He stopped and turned toward her.

She waited for him to continue.

"I'll speak with Thomas soon about a position in his office. Let me get my financial house in order, and then…" He looked down, shuffled his shoes on the pebbles, and looked back at her. "And then I will ask you to be my wife."

She rose to her tiptoes and kissed his cheek. "I shall wait for you, John. I shall do whatever it takes to become your wife."

* * *

On the warm spring morning of May 28, 1629, Katherine gave birth to a daughter. They named her Mary, and within the next few weeks, the family again descended upon the house to see the infant and wish the family well. After the bustle of what seemed like one hundred family members coming and going from the property for a month, the house was finally quiet. Everyone had gone home, and the only ones remaining were Katherine and the babe sleeping upstairs and Thomas and John sitting in front of the fireplace in the parlor.

"Do you remember her?" Thomas asked.

John nodded. "Yes, a little. I remember how much she loved us. She was always smiling and I remember her singing to us."

Thomas sipped his wine and stared into the fireplace. "Yes, that's what I remember also. Our mother was the kindest woman, not only to us but to everyone. She treated Mrs. Woodbury like she was her sister, and she loved our father more than life itself."

John's brow wrinkled. "You remember our father being present? That's the one thing I don't remember. I've given it a great amount of thought since being back in this house, but I don't ever remember our father being here when we were small."

"He wasn't very much. He was always away on business, but that's what made it possible for us to live such a grand lifestyle."

"That's not true, Thomas. Our grandfather and our cousins all lived this way and they weren't away from home for weeks and months on end."

Thomas placed his empty glass on the table next to him and sat up straight. "I don't know about that. Our grandfather was away working when he was young, and JC is never home. He's always off somewhere working in the king's service. You know, some people like nothing better than to work. I think our father is one of those people."

"He certainly enjoyed work more than spending time with us."

"I wouldn't put it that way."

"I would. I couldn't imagine having children and never seeing them."

Thomas chuckled. "Well, now that I have

that little baby upstairs, I understand that statement so well. I'm excited every morning just to see her shining little face. How I have fallen in love with that child. She has given my life a whole new meaning. At the same time, I would work tirelessly for the rest of my life to give her the best of everything, knowing that would come at the expense of never seeing her. I can't even describe to you what a tightrope this is to walk."

"I wonder if Father ever thought it a tightrope."

"John, our father loves us. He did the best he could."

"That's the same thing Mrs. Woodbury told me the morning Mother died. I will say the same thing to you I said to her—if that was his best, it wasn't good enough." John stared into the fireplace, contemplating ships and law and his father, and his future role as a husband and father. "I am happy for you and Katherine, and God willing, I hope to have children someday myself. You know, I think being a man includes sacrificing for what's important. I don't think it's about being selfish and doing what you want to do at the expense of those who love you."

"You, my dear brother, have grown up, but I wish you could understand that Father worked hard to give us a privileged life. He didn't work long hours because he didn't love us."

"I was talking more of me than of Father. I want to ask you a favor."

"Anything. Name it."

"I want to come to work for you as a clerk."

Thomas smiled. "I thought you'd never ask. Yes, I have a place for you in my law chambers, but I don't want you to be a clerk. I want you to be a lawyer."

"Really? I never thought I would warrant such a position."

"Nonsense. You are the brightest graduate to ever come out of Middle Temple, besides me, of course." Thomas laughed.

John laughed also. "And you're also the most modest."

Thomas got up and poured himself another glass of wine. He brought the carafe over and filled up John's glass, too. They clicked their glasses together and drank deeply.

"Thomas, lately I've come to the realization that you were the one who always looked after me. It was never Father. You taught me to tie my laces and to ride a horse. And it was you who helped me with Latin and mathematics so our tutor wouldn't think me senseless. You took care of me at home, and when we got older, you looked out for me when we went away to school. I find myself becoming more and more convinced that you are the one I owe everything to, and you are the one I want to make proud. I promise you I will be a good lawyer for your business. I've given up my dream of owning a ship. Mary has taken that place of importance in my life."

"I knew you'd figure it out eventually, little brother."

CHAPTER 23
October 1629,
The King and Parliament

Alexander arrived at Greenway Court on a cloudy and dreary afternoon. He had been invited to dine with the family and had ridden straight from London. He wished to speak with Thomas about the current political turmoil.

Thomas opened the door to greet him. "Uncle, it is so good to see you." Thomas hugged him, patted him on the back, and escorted him into the dining room.

Katherine entered the room from the library, looking elegant in her formal gown. Alexander looked down at his clothing, dusty from the four-hour ride. "I'm afraid I'm quite underdressed," he said.

"Nonsense. I'm happy to see you no matter what your attire. I'm glad you could come." Katherine kissed him on the cheek.

He looked down at her swollen belly and grinned. "I'm glad, too. How are you feeling?"

"This pregnancy is taking a lot more out of me than the first one did, but I'm doing all right."

She gestured to the seat on the end. "Please be seated, and I'll inform the staff that we're ready." She disappeared through the doorway as Alexander sat at the far end of the table.

When she came back into the room, he said, "Everything looks so formal." The table settings were of the finest silver plate.

"Well, we don't often have company for supper." Katherine smiled.

Alexander turned to Thomas. "I just came from London where I visited with John. He said to expect him home tomorrow."

"Thank you for the message," Thomas said.

"I heard there's some unrest in town. John's not involved in it, is he?" Katherine asked.

"No, of course not. When I left him, he was working quietly in his office."

The servants entered the room carrying overflowing platters of food. Turkey, sweet breads, an entire pheasant.

"Everything smells delicious," Thomas said.

"Help yourself, husband." Katherine grinned at him from the corner of the table as one of the servants began filling their glasses.

For the next hour, the trio dined and made small talk, but Alexander remained quiet, content with listening to Katherine tell him about little Mary's antics, and Thomas filling him in on the latest happenings at his law chambers.

After they finished eating, Alexander broached the subject he came to discuss. "I have been giving some thought to a serious matter that I wish to discuss with you, Thomas."

"Would you care to adjourn to the library,

Uncle?"

"We can talk here if Katherine doesn't mind. The topic concerns her also."

Katherine raised her eyebrows. "Well, then, by all means, discuss whatever you need to."

"Well, as you mentioned, there is unrest in London. Everyone is upset over Parliament being disbanded and those nine men being imprisoned."

"What exactly happened with those men, Uncle?" Katherine asked.

Alexander leaned back in his chair. He knew she didn't follow politics and he would have to start from the beginning for her to understand the turmoil facing the country. "Leading up to the unrest is a long story, but if you'll indulge me."

Katherine nodded.

"Just before Charles took the throne, you know he married Princess Henrietta Maria of France. Since her stance as a devout Catholic could be conceived as a potential threat to England, Charles delayed the opening of his first Parliament to avoid any opposition to the marriage."

"Yes, I remember that. It was quite a scandal," said Katherine.

"Well, during the same time, the king's close friend, the duke of Buckingham, was the leader of the English forces. In return for France's support against the Spanish, Buckingham offered seven English warships to help fight against the Protestants in France. The king needed to raise funds for this army, so he imposed a forced tax upon English citizens without Parliament's consent."

Thomas looked at Katherine and added, "The mere concept of Protestants funding a war against other Protestants provoked unrest in London, but the most important part is only Parliament can raise taxes. The king has no right to tax citizens."

Alexander nodded and continued. "Yes, and his subsequent action of imprisoning those who would not pay caused even more outrage. He was forced to convene Parliament in an attempt to ease the unrest."

"Why would Buckingham agree to an arrangement like that...against the Protestants, I mean?"

"I don't know, but it's just another in Buckingham's long list of military blunders. His attack on Cadiz ended with his troops coming across a warehouse of wine, and they opted to get drunk and return home instead of fighting."

Katherine giggled.

"The worst was his poorly executed siege on St. Martin-de-Ré, in which he lost more than four thousand men. So, when the king finally assembled Parliament, they did nothing but speak strongly against Buckingham's incompetence and demanded he be dismissed. The king, instead, dismissed Parliament."

Katherine rose and filled Alexander's wineglass. "I remember hearing about that."

He nodded a thank you, took a sip, and continued. "Well, last summer Buckingham was assassinated by one of his own men."

Katherine gasped.

"The king found himself with no leader to head his army and no way to fund them, so last month, he was again forced to convene Parliament. This is only the second time they've met since his coronation three years ago. In their distrust of the king's religious policies, they unanimously passed a resolution against Catholicism. The king was enraged and imprisoned nine of the leaders for passing a bill without his royal assent, then he dismissed the group for the second time."

"I can certainly understand why there is unrest in town," Katherine said.

"Well, the imprisonment of the men gave popular cause to their religious protest and has effectively turned them into martyrs. The unrest is escalating as protests are rising in the streets. If upstanding members of Parliament are being arrested, where is the protection for everyone else? Dissidents have begun meeting behind closed doors, even here in Kent." He looked at Thomas. "You know our family will support the king in all situations, just as we have always done, but I'm afraid if the tide turns, we will be at the mercy of Parliament."

"What do you mean, if the tide turns?" Thomas asked.

Alexander leaned forward. "I'm afraid there are rumblings of an uprising. If we go to war and we lose, well…" He shrugged.

"You think we'd going to war over this? The king governs according to his own conscience, and I think Parliament was out of order passing a resolution just to spite the queen. She's Catholic. No one can do anything about that."

"Yes, but she made a public display by not attending his coronation because it was held in a Protestant church. What kind of allegiance to the Crown is that? If anyone else behaved in such a manner, they'd be hung. She has shown her true colors, and the people are not happy about it."

"You're right, Uncle, but we all have our wives to deal with, don't we?" Thomas winked at Katherine across the table.

Alexander cleared his throat. "Your wife is the reason I wanted to speak with you."

"I don't understand." Thomas wrinkled his brow.

"Since I don't have any children of my own, I've decided to leave Leeds Castle to you in my will. If we end up going to war in support of the king and we lose, Parliament will seize all our lands, so we need to protect our property. I want to leave Leeds Castle in trust to your son. He will be a minor and not be involved in any sort of uprising, so Parliament won't be able to take anything that belongs to him. What do you think of that idea? It's legal, right?"

"Yes, it's legal, but I don't have a son yet. What happens if this coming child is also a girl?"

"Then I will postpone writing my will until you have a son, but it's important that you get busy in doing so. I'm not so young anymore. I'll be sixty-one this year."

Thomas laughed. "Uncle, I'll be happy to oblige in helping you get an heir."

Katherine playfully narrowed her eyes at her husband.

Alexander looked from one to the other. "May I ask one thing in exchange?"

"Of course," Thomas said.

"When you have a son, will you name him Alexander?"

Thomas smiled. "Yes, Alexander Culpepper

is a fine name."

CHAPTER 24
December 3, 1630

John stood in the doorway of the church and watched his father climb down from his carriage. Sporadic blasts of cold wind whipped at Johannes's thinning, gray hair and ruffled the hem of his cloak. He refused help from his footman and grunted with each movement. He was pale and wrinkled, his shoulders hunched by the weight of his sixty-five years. He leaned on his cane as he hobbled toward the church, favoring one leg over the other. When he reached the door, he looked up at John with tears in his bloodshot eyes. John stepped forward to take his father's arm and escort him inside.

As they stepped through the stone archway into the church, Johannes grumbled, "Bloody flux."

John nodded, not knowing if the comment required a reply. "Where's Ann?" he asked instead.

"She's visiting at her son's house. I didn't have time to go fetch her. I came straight here."

John nodded again. He led his father to the front pew and helped him be seated. John stood in front of the pew and looked around at the family in attendance. Mary and Cicely sat with Frances and her husband in the second row. Alexander and the St. Leger family sat on the other side of the church. JC and other Culpeppers sat behind Alexander. For the first time in John's life, he felt as if he needed to be the man in control of the family. This was an unusual sensation because his father or brother always filled the role of patriarch, but John accepted it for the time being. He returned to the door, just in time to see Thomas and Katherine enter.

Katherine was holding their eight-month-old baby Anna in her arms. John walked straight toward her, softly placed his hand on the infant's head, and looked into Katherine's eyes. "Katherine, I am so very sorry. Mary was such a beautiful little girl."

Katherine looked down at Anna. Her lip quivered and tears rolled down her cheeks.

"And little Anna is just as beautiful." John kissed the sleeping baby on the forehead.

"We had hoped for a son," said Thomas quietly, "but we were happy to have Anna as a playmate for Mary. Sometimes plans and dreams just don't work out." Thomas's voice cracked.

John understood that statement well. He looked into his brother's face and realized he had never seen his brother so sad. If he could figure out a way to take this pain from him, he would. Katherine began to sob, and the men escorted her to the front pew.

After a long and dismal hour, the sermon finally ended and the family gathered outside in the graveyard, surrounded by stone monuments and chiseled epitaphs. Blustery snowflakes wafted through the air, twirling around bare branches of dormant oaks, as the family placed young Mary

Culpepper in her tomb and solemnly left the grounds. John followed Thomas and Katherine home to Greenway Court. He left Johannes to fend for himself.

CHAPTER 25
1631, Leeds Castle

The following year, Thomas and Katherine celebrated the birth of their third child, the son they had been hoping for. They named him Alex at Alexander's request. After the child's baptism at St. John the Baptist Church, the family gathered at Leeds Castle for a celebration. All the Culpeppers and St. Legers were in attendance, including Katherine's ship-commanding father, Warham, who had not been seen on dry land for several years. The man had the sea in his blood, and even when he docked his ship in the Thames, he seldom ventured inland for long. He stayed at the wharf, resupplying his ship for his next expedition.

His face was brown, weathered by the wind and the sun. He looked like a dried-up piece of leather. Although Warham was baby Alex's grandfather by blood, Alexander was the one who pranced around the castle most of the afternoon, holding his namesake in his arms. This was as close as Alexander would ever come to having a grandson.

"Warham, how good to see you again." John shook Warham's callused hands.

"You too, John. How are things in the legal world?"

"Just fine. How are things in the sailing world?"

"I keep myself busy. Whatever became of your sailing desires? I remember hearing that as a young lad, you always talked about sailing someday. Are you still planning to take to the sea or are you going to stay on land?"

"That's a long and complicated story that I won't bore you with, but I plan on remaining in London for now." John leaned toward Warham and whispered. "I'd still love to sail someday, but don't tell anyone I said that."

Warham laughed.

John sipped his wine. "Do you have time to tell me about some of your adventures?"

"Oh, that's a sore subject," Warham said.

"It certainly is," Alexander said, standing nearby. Baby Alex stirred in his arms. "If you'll excuse me, I think this little one needs his mother."

Alexander disappeared through the archway.

"Why is sailing a sore subject?" John asked.

Warham took a gulp of his wine and gestured around the room. "Well, I inherited this grand estate from my father when he died, but after I sailed with Sir Raleigh and didn't make the profit I was expecting, I could no longer support the ship and the crew. I lost everything in that expedition. I had a choice to sell my ship or my house. My mother talked your uncle into buying Leeds Castle because they were living here and didn't want to be uprooted. I was pleased that he was kind enough to help me out, but I think he always felt as if he was solely financing my expeditions. There's been a bit of tension between us since that time."

"I seem to remember something about that. I didn't realize you had to sell the castle to support your ship."

"Sailing is an expensive hobby."

"What happened to the expedition?"

"Well, Raleigh was not quite an upstanding citizen. At King James's request, we sailed to Guiana in search of El Dorado's gold, which Raleigh said he could find because he had seen it before. But when we got there, we didn't even get the chance to find it. He commanded us to attack the Spanish outpost of Santo Tomé, which was in violation of the English treaty with Spain, so by the time we returned to London, the Spanish ambassador had reached the king first and demanded justice. Raleigh was arrested and executed. He was quite a sailor, though. The sea agreed with him. Too bad Spain didn't agree with him."

"What about the gold?"

Warham took another drink of his wine and shook his head. "We never found it. Hence my having to sell my family's home."

John wrinkled his forehead. "The expedition was that expensive?"

"Supporting a ship of sailors costs a lot of money, so my word of advice to you is if you plan on owning a ship, make sure you have big pockets, and whatever you do, don't mention your desire to own a ship to any of the men in your family."

"Too late. I've already attracted their wrath, especially my father's."

"Well, your father lost a huge sum of money

to the Virginia Company. I think he single-handedly supported the colony at Jamestown for an entire decade. I don't even know how much your uncle Tom lost, but he was completely broke the last few years of his life."

"Well, at least Leeds Castle will return to your family, since Alexander is passing it down to your grandson."

"Yes, there is some solace in that, but having to sell it for business losses was a heartbreaking event in the first place. It didn't sit well with anyone involved. I'm still bitter about having to sell it, and your uncle is still bitter about having to buy it."

"Well, I was hoping for better news about the ship business, but I'm glad you told me the whole story, good and bad. I guess I made the right decision becoming a lawyer."

"On the other side of the coin, that expedition was the best time of my life. The sea holds many possibilities and you'll never feel more alive than when sailing the ocean, heading to an unknown destination. The sun, the spray, the smells. It's always a great adventure."

John felt a deep twinge of jealousy and was glad the conversation had concluded as Mary approached them.

John smiled and placed his hand on the small of her back. "Mary, my dear, have you met Katherine's father? This is Warham St. Leger."

"Hello, Mr. St. Leger. I've heard of your sailing adventures. It's a pleasure to finally meet you."

"It's a great honor to meet you, madam. I was just telling John about my excursion with Sir

Walter Raleigh."

"Don't tell him the good parts. I just got him to settle down here in London."

Warham looked at John and smirked. "Well, that explains why you've given up your dream of sailing. There's room for only one mistress in a man's life, and apparently this beautiful lady is yours."

Mary smiled and John laughed at the good-natured teasing, but his heart felt heavy. He would give almost anything to sail with Warham—anything except Mary, of course.

The next morning, Alexander summoned Thomas and John to his office to witness the writing of his will, leaving Leeds Castle in trust to baby Alex.

CHAPTER 26
1632, Astwood Court

John galloped onto the grounds of his father's estate, his horse crunching through the fallen leaves. He had ridden for six days through gold and red trees, across fields of brown, and streams that were becoming colder with each passing fall day. He was happy to finally arrive at Astwood Court. He left his horse untethered on the front lawn and ran into the house, calling for Mary. He shouted her name over and over but received no response. He called for his father, for Cicely, for Ann. There wasn't even a servant in the house to greet him.

He ran up the stairs and went from room to room, finding each vacant. He searched the parlor and the library. He even walked back to the kitchen but found only an empty fireplace with a pot of cold porridge hanging from the iron handle. He walked out to the stable to look for his father's carriage, but it wasn't there.

"Boy," he yelled to the stable hand, "where is everyone?"

"Master Culpepper took m'lady and Mistress Cicely into town. Mistress Mary is here. I believe she's on the back terrace," the dirty-faced boy answered.

John ran back through the house and emerged onto the back terrace. He found Mary reading a book in the warmth of the sunshine. Her feet, covered in dainty slippers, were propped up on the edge of a chair. She looked up in surprise and quickly pulled her feet down. A smile spread across her face.

"John Culpepper! What a nice surprise!" She rose, placing her book on her chair, and floated toward him in her peach dress.

He reached for her hands and kissed her on both cheeks.

"I've come on very important business."

"Oh, I'm sorry, your father isn't here. He took Ann and Cicely into town to do some shopping. They won't be home for a few days."

"I didn't come to speak with him. I came to speak with you." He held on tightly to her hands.

"Me? Whatever for?"

He didn't move for a moment, his boots glued to the stone patio.

"What is it, John? Is everything all right?"

He looked across the yard as he assembled the words, and then looked into her eyes. "I've been thinking it's time for us to move forward with our lives. I've decided to open my own chambers in London. I'm ready to settle down."

He knelt down on one knee and Mary gasped. She pulled her hand from his and placed it on her chest.

"Mary, I knew I loved you the first time we met. I don't want anything more in the world than to spend my life with you. Would you do me the honor of becoming my wife?"

The biggest smile he had ever seen crossed her face. "Of course I will."

He rose, wrapped her in his arms, and kissed her.

"Your family will be so excited," she gushed. "You're going to open your own law office?"

"Yes, I am."

She wrapped her arms around his neck. "Your father is going to be thrilled."

"Can we not talk about him right now?"

"I'm sorry, John. I just want you to be happy."

"I am happy…when I'm with you." He kissed her again.

When their embrace ended, she asked, "Well, Mr. Culpepper, when should we marry?"

"How about right now?"

"Now? I don't even have a suitable dress."

"You look beautiful in the dress you're wearing. I want you to be my wife, I want to start a family, and I want to do so this very moment."

The two young lovers rode to the nearest church and pounded on every door until they found someone to marry them. They spent the next two days alone at Astwood Court planning their future.

CHAPTER 27
1633 Henry Culpepper

Mary and John moved into Greenway Court with Thomas's family so John could be closer to London and his newly opened law practice. He found it impossible to ride into town, work all day, and travel back home, so he spent days at a time in town and was saddened by every moment away from his wife. As his practice grew, he couldn't return home more than once per week, and then only for a day or so. Over the course of the four-hour journey he made twice per week, he had plenty of time to mull over his childhood and his absentee father. He hadn't realized the sacrifice his father had made until he had to do it himself. By the fiftieth journey, he forgave the man just a bit for not being home most of the time.

Nine months after moving to Greenway Court, Mary gave birth to a healthy baby boy with blue-gray eyes and dark curly hair like his father. He was baptized Henry Culpepper at All Saint's Church in Hollingbourne. John thought having a son would be a thrilling experience and the final brick in the life he was building, but in truth, it put more pressure on him than he could handle. He wasn't in line to inherit the Culpepper wealth, so if he was to leave anything substantial to his son, he would have to work harder and create his own wealth. He wanted to be home with Mary and watch his son grow, but he felt forced to spend more time in London, more time working a job that made him increasingly unhappy. He was miserable at work. He was restless at home.

A few months after Henry's birth, John found Mary sitting at the dining room table holding the baby, her forehead furrowed.

"What's wrong, Mary? Is something on your mind?" John asked, unaccustomed to seeing his wife with a perplexed look on her face.

"I just spoke with Katherine, and she said Thomas was promoted to colonel in the king's army. Since the king refuses Parliament's request to reconvene and there's so much unrest in town, I'm very concerned about the future of our country." She gently bounced Henry in her arms.

John placed his cup of cider on the table and sat down across from his wife. "It's worrisome to wonder what's going to happy next. Thomas said the king knows of the growing unrest and that's why he's expanding his army. But I promise you that you and Henry are safe at Greenway Court. Nothing is going to happen way out here in the country."

"What about your safety in London?"

John smiled. "I can take care of myself, but I am grateful for your concern."

* * *

The Culpepper men—Thomas, John, Johannes, JC, and Alexander—met the following week for supper at Greenway Court to discuss the unrest.

"We need to make it very clear whose side we're on," said Alexander.

"It's always been clear, brother. The Culpeppers back the monarchy. We always have and we would never stand behind an illegal Parliament," said Johannes.

"What makes them illegal?" asked John.

The other men snickered at him as if he were a small schoolboy and not a lawyer. Thomas was the one to answer. "If the king disbanded Parliament, there is no Parliament. They work for the king and they only exist if he says so."

"But they exist to protect the interest of the people," John said.

"Not under *this* king's rule," Johannes grumbled. "He holds himself to rule by divine right, and no one can usurp his royal prerogative, especially Parliament."

JC added, "Well, there's something brewing. This morning I was asked to remain available in case the king wants me to escort the queen to the Netherlands for safekeeping."

"It's become so bad they want to send the queen away?" asked John.

Thomas nodded. "The king knows something serious is coming."

"He does, and he's nervous about it," JC said. "But no matter what happens, we stand with him."

Thomas raised his mug of ale. "Long live the king."

The men cheered and drank. John stared into his mug.

"What is it, John?" Thomas asked.

"Do you really think we're going to war?"

Alexander nodded solemnly. "War is coming. You can be assured of that."

CHAPTER 28
Summer 1633,
Greenway Court

John sat on the back terrace and stared at the black sky that was turning dark shades of purple with the rising sun. He hadn't been home for the last month, and now that he was here for a few days, he was anxious to get back to London. More and more, he was finding at work that he wanted to be home, and when he was home, he needed to be at work. More than anything, he longed to be at sea.

"Good morning, husband," Mary said as she emerged from the house. She sat down in the chair next to him.

"Good morning." He continued staring straight ahead at the horizon.

"Is something troubling you this morning?"

"I've just been thinking about the state of the country. Thomas is serving in the king's army, JC is talking of escorting the queen to the Netherlands, and Uncle Alexander never leaves the king's side these days. The citizens are ready to go to war, and the king is ready to have every one of them beheaded. I don't know why men fight like this. I wish we could live our lives in peace."

"I've been thinking the same thing. Not so much for us, but for Henry."

John looked at her and smiled. "How is my curly-headed boy this morning?"

"He's still sleeping. You're missing so many of his antics. He's smiling now and trying to roll over. I wish you could spend more time with him, John."

"I wish I could, too, but even with the unrest, people still need lawyers."

"I'm not sure it's my place to say, but it seems Henry is growing up without his father just like you did."

John's jaw twitched as he clenched his teeth. He *had* been busy with work but he'd been doing it for his son.

Mary sensed his displeasure. "John, I'm sorry. I know you're doing what's best for the family. I shouldn't have brought it up."

"It's all right. I know I haven't been here very much, but there's nothing I can do about it. At least I'm in the country."

"What does that mean?" She tried to make it sound like an innocent question, but it held a tone of harshness she couldn't disguise.

"I'm not sailing the world as I wish. I'm a lawyer. I'm at home as much as I'm going to be," he snapped. He thought he should stop the words from flowing out, but he couldn't.

Mary sighed and looked across the grounds, watching birds swoop over the horizon as the sky turned to brilliant shades of red and pink. "Would you like to be at sea?"

"You know I would. That's been my dream for as long as I can remember."

She lifted her skirt and rose from her chair. She stepped in front of John and looked down into his eyes. "I sincerely thought you'd be happy as a husband and a father."

He started to interrupt her, but she placed her hand up for him to stop. "Let me say this, please."

He nodded for her to continue.

"You have been miserable and depressed since the day we married. I thought once we had a child, you would ease into family life, but even Henry has not been able to bring the smile back to your face. I'm not a selfish woman, John. I want you to be happy. That's the only thing that's important to me." She looked at the ground.

He waited for her to continue, knowing she was right. He had been acting like a spoiled child, but he was unhappy. His childhood wishes had been nothing but a dream, a notion that had disappeared in a puff of smoke. He hated his life, he hated London, he hated being a lawyer.

She swallowed hard. "If sailing a vessel is what you long to do, please do it."

"Are you trying to get rid of me?" He laughed, attempting to ease the tension, but she didn't join him.

"No, John, I'm not trying to get rid of you. I'm telling you to be happy. Even when you're home, you're sullen and withdrawn. I don't want you to stay here because you promised me you would. I don't want to be the cause of your distress. But I do want you to know one very important thing. If you decide to sail a ship, I will be here waiting when you return, and I expect you to return with a smile on your face."

The pink sky behind her had transformed to sapphire blue, giving her hair a silky sheen. She was the most beautiful, intelligent, and kind woman he had ever known and he was lucky to have her. He rose from his chair, wrapped his arms around her waist, and kissed her lips. "I'll give it some thought. Perhaps I can find a way to make my dreams come true." He kissed her again. "I promise you, if I go, I will come home to you. I, John Culpepper, will always come home to you."

Later that day, John found Thomas upstairs in his office.

"Ah, brother, are you going into town today? I need someone to deliver this correspondence to London," Thomas said before John had even said hello.

"I'd be happy to deliver them, but I'd like to speak to you about something first if I may."

"Of course. What's on your mind?"

"I've decided to buy a ship."

Thomas stopped writing and looked up. "I thought you had decided to be a good lawyer and a good husband."

John pulled a chair across the floor and placed it in front of his brother. He sat on the edge of it, his elbows resting on Thomas's desk. "Thomas, did you ever have a dream so big that you couldn't let it go?"

"Yes, I always wanted to become a well-respected lawyer like our father and our grandfather."

"What if everyone told you your dream was rubbish and that you'd never be able to accomplish it? What if everyone told you to be a janitor instead?"

"A janitor? That's ridiculous."

"Yes, it is ridiculous. You could no more be a janitor than I can be a lawyer. I hate every minute of debating policies and shuffling papers. I want to be a ship's captain. I've wanted that since I was a child. You know. You were there." He looked out the diamond-shaped panes of the window. "I've wanted to travel the world since I can remember—see new things, experience new adventures, do things no one in our family has ever done before. I want to hear the snap of the sails and feel the ocean spray on my face. I want to sail away and return a hero."

"Well, I admit, I haven't seen you this excited in a long time. What does Mary say about this?"

John looked back at him. "She gave me her blessing."

"She did?" Thomas raised his eyebrows in surprise.

John nodded.

Thomas sighed. "So, what do you want from me?"

"I need help with the financing. I have enough money to buy half a ship. I need the other half."

Thomas's face grew serious as he looked down at his desk. "You know I'd do anything for you. You're my only brother."

"Then you'll help me?"

He looked back up and nodded. "Father is going to kill me, but yes, I'll help you."

John grinned. "I know Father will disapprove, but this is my life, not his."

"Well, you have to tell him yourself. I'm not going to."

"Very well. I'll send him word once I purchase a ship. I'll invite him to come to London and see it."

"He won't come."

"That's his choice." John picked up the correspondence that needed to be delivered and rose. "I'll deliver these before I start shopping for a ship." He walked toward the door.

"John," Thomas called. "Good luck. I hope this makes you happy."

John stopped with his hand on the brass doorknob and turned to face his brother. "I'm already happy."

CHAPTER 29
1633, London

John searched tirelessly for months and eventually ended up at a shipyard on the English Channel. When he first laid eyes on her, he knew she was the one. She was a Dutch fluyt, specifically designed for carrying cargo across the ocean. Her pear shape featured a block-and-tackle pulley system that would come in handy loading and unloading her. She had three masts, her sails were wrapped tightly around her yardarms, and the red-and-white flag of England fluttered atop her mainmast. After speaking with her owner, learning she had sailed the ocean many times, and finding she was reasonably priced, John bought her without even taking her out to sea. He paid to have her navigated up to London, and a week after she arrived, he took Thomas down to the dockyard to see her.

"She's a shallow draught," said John as they climbed down from their wagon.

"I don't know what that means," said Thomas.

"It means she sits shallow in the water, allowing her to dock in ports and rivers that other ships can't reach."

Thomas followed John as he scurried through sailors and dockworkers on the busy wharf. When they approached the ship's berth, they saw a haggard old man sitting on a plank that was hanging by ropes off her aft.

"Hello, Mr. Trowbridge," John yelled to the man.

"Hello, Mr. Culpepper. I've just finished painting." The toothless man proceeded to hoist himself back onto the upper deck.

Thomas stopped dead in his tracks when he saw what the old man was painting. John spun around to look at his brother's stunned face.

"Well, what do you think?" John asked, his smile huge.

Thomas's eyes filled with delight. On the back of the ship, ornate white letters read *Thomas and John*. "It's amazing. She is impressive indeed and her name says it all."

"I knew you'd approve." John bounced toward the gangplank, as excited as a child with a new toy. "Come look at the inside. She's a beauty." Once he boarded, he turned to Thomas, who had followed him up the gangplank. "She can sail with a crew of only twelve."

"It only takes twelve people to operate this thing?"

John nodded as he pointed up at the mainmast. "Because her sails are smaller, it doesn't take as many men to set them. See? It's a square rig with room for three sails. She's impressively fast."

For two hours, John told Thomas the names of each sail and rope and explained how they all worked. He showed Thomas every corner and crevasse of their new ship.

"You know more about ships than you do about law," Thomas said.

"Well, I've studied them longer." John laughed. He stood in the middle of the deck, looked around, and became quiet as the idea of owning this ship struck him for the very first time. He froze and smiled with pride.

"You look like you belong here," Thomas said.

John threw his hands up to shoulder level, palms facing upward. "Have you ever seen anything more beautiful in all your life?"

Thomas walked across the deck and gave him a quick hug. "I'm very happy for you, John. Did you invite Father to come see her?"

"You have to ruin my good mood by speaking of that old man?"

"Yes, I do. Did you invite him?"

"Yes, but Ann sent a message that he's ill and won't come."

"Won't or can't?"

"I don't know." John reached down and picked up the end of a rope.

"Did she say if he said anything about the ship?"

"No." John coiled the rope.

"How ill is he?"

"She didn't say, only that the doctor was coming to see him because he's bedridden."

"Do you think we should go see him?"

John blew a puff of air from his lips and dropped the coiled rope off to the side. "Did he ever take the time to come see us?"

"John, you have to let this go. You know he was always working."

"All I know is he was never there for us, and I'm not wasting my time traveling out to see him. I invited him to come see my ship. If he doesn't want to, that's up to him."

Thomas sighed, knowing he could never settle the rift between his brother and his father. They had been adversaries for nearly twenty-seven years. Too much time had passed for their dispute to ever be resolved. There was too much pride in his father, too much heartache in his brother, and too much stubbornness in them both. They were exactly alike, though they would both adamantly disagree.

Thomas found it curious that John was going to sail away for months, perhaps even years, and leave his son Henry. He wondered if John realized he was going to be absent just like his own father, whom he resented. Thomas looked at John and decided to broach the subject at a later date. Today was John's day to shine. His eyes held an excitement Thomas hadn't seen since the day they watched the *Mayflower* sail away. John looked like he was fourteen all over again. The only thing Thomas knew for sure was that he would do his best to look after Mary and Henry until John returned.

Thomas smiled at his little brother and patted him on the back. "Congratulations, John. Your dream has finally come true."

CHAPTER 30
1634,
Destination
Virginia Colony

Thomas, Mary, and one-year-old Henry arrived at the dock at daybreak on the morning John was to set sail. John had spent the last month at the dockyard supplying his ship and hiring his crew. He had barely seen his wife since he bought the ship, so he asked Thomas to bring Mary and Henry to the dock early so he could spend some time with them before he sailed. After dropping them off, Thomas left, saying he had an important errand to run.

Two hours later, Thomas reappeared on the dock with an elderly woman on his arm. They slowly walked across the dusty road and John saw them coming from a distance. He recognized her immediately and ran to greet them.

"Mrs. Woodbury!" He wrapped his arms around her, and she hugged him for a long time. She was thin and frail, not the plump governess he remembered.

"John, my boy. Look at you! You are a grown

man." Tears of joy filled her eyes.

"What are you doing here?" he asked.

"Thomas told me about your ship, and I couldn't let you sail away without seeing it for myself. You've talked about nothing but owning a ship your whole life."

"Well, come look at her. She's magnificent." He took Mrs. Woodbury's arm and escorted her to the ship.

Standing on the dock, she nodded as John told her all about the ship, but she had trouble taking her eyes off the young woman sitting on a wooden crate on the dirt, bouncing a toddler on her lap. "Is that Mary?"

"Oh, yes, that's Mary and my son Henry," John answered. He took Mrs. Woodbury over to greet them. The old woman hugged and kissed both of them.

"Mary, my dear, I remember you so fondly. I'd heard you and John married, and now you have a son. I'm so pleased for you both."

"Thank you, Mrs. Woodbury. It is indeed a pleasure to see you again," said Mary.

Thomas said, "Mary, would you like to go for a walk and leave John and Mrs. Woodbury to talk for a bit?"

Mary nodded and lifted Henry onto her hip, and they strolled down the dock.

After they left, Mrs. Woodbury's expression became serious. "John, I wanted to speak with you before you left. Thomas told me you invited your father to come see your ship, but he wasn't able to make the trip."

"I heard he is ill, but even if he wasn't, I'm

sure he still wouldn't come."

"You've always thought the worst of your father."

"He's never been supportive of me. I'm not surprised or saddened by his absence."

She sat down on the wooden crate where Mary had been sitting. "But you're angry."

How did she always know what he was feeling?

"John, have a seat and let's talk for a minute."

John dragged another crate across the ground and placed it in front of her. He sat down with his elbows resting on his knees and looked at her. Even though she had aged more than a decade and the lines on her face were much deeper than he remembered, her eyes were the same and he was instantly transported back to his childhood.

"I was in the room the day you and your father met for the first time. I'd never before seen a man fall instantly in love with a baby. He stared at you and you stared right back at him and I know the rest of the world vanished at that moment for him. He touched your hand and you, only days old, grabbed his finger and wouldn't let go. We all know Johannes Culpepper is not a man to laugh out loud, but you made him laugh that day. You made him happier than I had ever seen him."

John wondered why he had never heard this story before.

"I was the only one in the room with him and your mother, and I will tell you beyond the shadow of any doubt that your father loves you more than anything."

John stretched out his legs and crossed his ankles. He looked at the ground and the corners of his lips turned down. "He has a strange way of showing love."

"You don't understand your father's intentions. When Thomas was a baby, he was a sickly child. None of us thought he'd survive past a few years. Then you came along, and you were healthy and bright eyed. Your father thought you would be his heir, his legacy. You would be the one thing that made his life worth living. He worked day and night for you, as you stood to inherit everything. He wanted you to follow in his footsteps, to become a lawyer so you could manage the family's estates. He didn't pamper you. He raised you to be strong so you could handle anything. From the moment you were born, he groomed you for the day he would no longer be here, the day you would become the Culpepper patriarch."

She paused to let him absorb what she was saying.

After a long while, he spoke. "I always thought he loved Thomas more than me and I was just a thorn in his side."

"Well, you certainly were a thorn. You were so headstrong, you destroyed his plans, refused to follow his path. You had your own mind and your own dreams. He would never admit it to you, but he was quite jealous of your strength. You see, I knew Johannes when he was a boy. He never wanted to follow in his father's footsteps either. His father was a lawyer, but Johannes never wanted to be one. He wanted to run a farm. He loved the open fields and the animals. He was more comfortable around animals than he was around people, that's why he sounded gruff so often. He didn't know how to talk to people. Since he was old enough to walk, he loved being in the barn more than being in the house. As a matter of fact, he was birthing a calf the morning your mother died."

"He was?"

She nodded.

"Why did he end up becoming a lawyer?" John asked.

"Because he didn't have the strength to stand up to his father. He didn't have the power you have. He envies that trait in you."

"Envies?"

"Yes, you are everything he always wanted to be. He has a hard time showing his feelings, but you, my boy, are his greatest love. He's certainly not perfect and perhaps wasn't the best father, but he has loved you from the first moment he laid eyes on you until this very day. I know he's sad that he isn't here today to see you off. He might not smile or pat you on the back, but deep in his heart, he is proud of you for following your dreams. I know he wishes he could show you his love, but he thinks you hate him."

"Maybe I do," John mumbled.

"Maybe you should reconsider."

John looked at her.

"Johannes is a stubborn man, and you are more like him than you care to admit."

John jutted his chin out. "Well, I'm not leaving my son forever. I'll be back in a few months."

"Your father never thought he was leaving

you forever, either. He knew he'd be home in a few days or a few weeks. I know you love Henry with all your heart, and Johannes feels the same way about you, only with twenty-seven years more experience."

John wiped a tear from his face. "Do you really think he'd be proud of me today?"

"I know he's proud of you." She gestured for him to help her up so she could give him a hug. After she released him, she said, "I'm proud of you, too."

Thomas and the ladies stood on the dock and watched the crew cast off the mighty ship's ropes. John stood proudly on the bow and bellowed to his crew to raise the sails. His curly brown hair tangled in his collar as it wafted in the breeze and his smile was radiant. Mary smiled through her tears as she waved good-bye. John held a taut rope with one hand and blew her a dramatic kiss with the other, and she pretended to catch it. He pointed to Mrs. Woodbury and mouthed, "Thank you." Mrs. Woodbury smiled and waved back.

Thomas wrapped his arm around Mary's shoulder. "He'll be back before you know it, Mary."

"I know he will."

"This has been his dream for as long as I can remember."

"I know, and I'm happy for him." She sniffled.

When the ship sailed out of sight, Thomas escorted the ladies home.

John stood on the bow for a long time, wondering if he was doing the right thing, yet his heart was filled with so much excitement, he thought it might explode. He looked up and watched a couple seagulls swooping around the sails. He would return home soon. He would come back to Mary and Henry. He might even go visit his father. He loved his family, but he had to do this. He had to sail across the ocean at least once in his lifetime. He trembled with anticipation as the wind whistled across the bow.

The ship rode the waves through the English Channel and emerged into the blue ocean. She lifted and fell with the swell, her sails billowing and straining against their ropes as they filled with wind. John felt his heart filling too, billowing and straining like a caged animal yearning for freedom. He was finally free, finally out on the open sea, and sailing to the new world would be his greatest adventure. He would return a different man, a hero sharing stories of settlers and Indians and amazing adventures. He gazed straight ahead, the salty spray cooling his face. The horizon was endless—no land, no houses, no steeples, no trees to block the view. It was a wide-open canvas. So was his future.

He thought of the last words spoken to him by his elderly grandfather: "Follow your heart no matter where it takes you. Be brave and fearless. The future has great things in store for you."

"Yes, it does, Grandfather. Yes, it does."

THE END

Author's Notes

This book stems from decades of genealogical research by me and others. I found that in the late 1500s, there were more than a dozen Culpepper barons and earls living in England. They had enormous wealth, vast land holdings, and great manor houses, many of which are still standing today. This was the privilege John Culpepper was born into. I wondered how and why, when they possessed such great power and prestige, they chose to sail across the ocean, move to an inhospitable land, and face possible starvation and death. Why would they leave the comfort of their manors and servants to live in probable squalor and battle savage Indians? How did they end up becoming the modest people I knew in my youth in Mississippi?

As I researched the family to find which one came to America first, I ran into the problem most Culpepper researchers run into. Each man named John had a brother named Thomas. Each John and Thomas had sons named John and Thomas. As the family grew, cousins and second cousins were all named John and Thomas, and they occasionally married within the family, creating a whole new tangled web of Culpepper history. The records blurred. The history became confusing. English records were destroyed. Colonial records were incomplete. After committing the known timelines of all of the different Johns and Thomases to paper, I believe I have sorted out which one was which. In an attempt to keep them straight in the reader's mind, I have given some of them nicknames, yet they are all listed in historical records as John or Thomas. Of course, as new documents are uncovered, it is possible that my theory is just as mistaken as theories that have come before.

John Culpepper the Merchant was the first in the family to migrate to America, and as I began unraveling English and colonial history, I found the answers to the above questions of how and why they ended up in America, along with shocking tales of what happened to them once they arrived and what happened to the ones left behind. This four-book series begins on the day John was born and ends at the end of his life, but John's is not the only story here. There are far too many religious and political events and bold and brave personalities surrounding the family to ignore. These events and people shaped the man we know as John Culpepper. This series uncovers a life of passion, heroism and bravery, love and forgiveness, and ultimately truth. Truth of our history and truth about life itself.

John Culpepper is believed to be the progenitor of all American Culpeppers. He was my tenth great-grandfather.

My deepest thanks go out to those who made this book possible:

Elyse Dinh-McCrillis—TheEditNinja.com

Robert Hess—book designer

Warren Culpepper and Lew Griffin, who maintain the Culpepper Connections website, and all of the Culpepper descendants who contribute to it.

References

www.CulpepperConnections.com

Culpeppers of England and America
by Warren H. (Dick) Culpepper

History of the Middle Temple
Edited by Richard O. Havery

Pioneers of the Old South:
A Chronical of English Colonial Beginnings
by Mary Johnson

Books by Lori Crane

Culpepper Saga

I, John Culpepper
John Culpepper the Merchant
John Culpepper, Esquire
Culpepper's Rebellion

Okatibbee Creek Series

Okatibbee Creek
An Orphan's Heart
Elly Hays

Stuckey's Bridge Trilogy

The Legend of Stuckey's Bridge
Stuckey's Legacy: The Legend Continues
Stuckey's Gold: The Curse of Lake Juzan

Other Books

Savannah's Bluebird
Witch Dance
The Culpepper-Fairfax Scandal
*On This Day: A Perpetual Calendar for Family
Genealogy*

About the Author

Bestselling and award-winning author Lori Crane is a writer of southern historical fiction and the occasional thriller. Her books have climbed to the Kindle Top 100 lists many times, with *Elly Hays* debuting on Amazon at #1 in Native American stories. She has also enjoyed a place among her peers in the Top 100 historical fiction authors on Amazon, climbing to #23. She is a native Mississippi belle currently residing in greater Nashville.

She is a member of the Daughters of the American Revolution, the United States Daughters of 1812, the United Daughters of the Confederacy, and the Historical Novel Society. She is also a profession musician and member of the Screen Actors Guild-American Federation of Television and Radio Artists.

Visit Lori's website at
www.LoriCrane.com

Excerpt from

John Culpepper
the Merchant

The second book in The Culpepper Saga

CHAPTER 1
January 4, 1642,
London, England

The king marched into the room unannounced. He walked through the middle of the active session of Parliament and was greeted with stunned silence. Never before had a monarch entered the House of Commons uninvited, and the nearly two hundred members present froze in place as if someone had painted their portrait, capturing the moment complete with paper strewn across tables, pens held in the air, and faces turned to pose for the painter. The king did not return their shocked gazes.

From his seat at a table in the center of the room, JC watched the king walk past him, easily slipping between the unmoving members of the House. JC's jaw fell open when the king sat in the speaker's chair. JC looked back toward the door, wondering how the king had entered the room without warning and saw the king's sergeant at arms blocking the doorway. Behind the intimidating man stood the king's soldiers— hundreds of them as far as JC could tell.

After a lengthy and excruciating silence, the king rose from the chair. The knuckles of his right hand turned white as he gripped the ball on top of his walking stick. His left hand remained at his side, balled into a fist.

"Gentlemen!" The king narrowed his eyes as he scrutinized each face. It was obvious he was not going to stay as he had neglected to remove his wide-brimmed hat, which matched his black velvet cloak. Underneath, he wore a red doublet and breeches, almost the same shade as his face. "I am sorry to have this occasion to come unto you, and I apologize for violating your parliamentary privilege." His beard twitched as he clenched his teeth. "But those guilty of treason have no privilege."

There was a collective gasp from the room, and a trickle of sweat dripped down JC's back. Parliament had not been convened for nearly nine years, as the king thought it his royal prerogative to rule the country alone, but after Scotland had invaded the north in retaliation for the king's religious rulings, he desperately needed money to fund his army. The only body that could legally raise taxes to fund an army was Parliament, so the king was forced to call on it. It denied the king's request to raise taxes, and instead compiled a list of over two hundred grievances against the king, demanding he address them. The document had been delivered a month ago but Parliament had never received word as to the king's reaction.

JC had not participated in the writing of the grievances. For the last nineteen years, he had worked in the king's service, just as his family had done for many kings and many generations. He would never contribute to anything as treasonous as telling the king how to rule. During his service, JC had never seen the king's demeanor this threatening. This unannounced visit to the House of Commons was not going to end well for someone.

The king lifted his hand and gestured for his sergeant at arms to enter the room.

All heads turned toward the door, and all eyes

followed the sergeant as he walked to the middle of the room and unrolled a piece of paper. He held it with both hands in front of his face and turned clockwise as he read aloud. "I am commanded by His Majesty, my master, upon my allegiance that I should come to the House of Commons and request from Mr. Speaker five members of the House of Commons. When these gentlemen are delivered, I am commanded to arrest them in His Majesty's name for high treason. Their names are Mr. Denzil Hollis, Sir Arthur Haselrig, Mr. John Pym, Mr. William Strode, and Mr. John Hampden."

The sergeant rolled up the paper and stuffed it back into his breast pocket.

JC witnessed a scowl cross the king's face while the sergeant read the names. The five men were the authors of the list of grievances.

"Mr. William Lenthall," the king bellowed.

A man wearing a black cape with a white collar emerged from the crowd and knelt before the king. "Yes, Your Majesty."

"Mr. Speaker, where are these men we seek? Do you see them in this room?"

Lenthall kept his eyes to the floor. "May it please Your Majesty, I have neither eyes to see nor tongue to speak in this place but only as the House is pleased to direct me, whose servant I am."

The king stared at the top of Lenthall's head. Lenthall remained still. No man risked a glance toward another or even dared to breathe for fear of attracting the king's attention. The king sighed and said, "I see all the birds have flown."

With a flick of his wrist, the king flipped his long hair off his shoulder and marched past Lenthall, leaving him kneeling in front of his own empty chair. The sergeant at arms followed the king from the room.

When the door slammed, everyone exhaled.

www.ingramcontent.com/pod-product-compliance
Lightning Source LLC
Chambersburg PA
CBHW071149170626
46809CB00002B/838